THE LITTLE WORLD OF DON CAMILLO

THE LITTLE WORLD OF DON CAMILLO

by GIOVANNI GUARESCHI

Translated from the Italian
by UNA VINCENZO TROUBRIDGE

IMAGE BOOKS
A Division of Doubleday & Company, Inc.
Garden City, New York
1986

Image Book edition published September 1986 by special arrangement with Farrar, Straus & Giroux, Inc.

Library of Congress Cataloging-in-Publication Data

Guareschi, Giovanni, 1908–1968.
The little world of Don Camillo.

Translation of: Mondo piccolo, Don Camillo.
I. Title.
PQ4817.U193M63 1986 853'.912 86-8845
ISBN: 0-385-23242-X

CONTENTS

HOW I GOT THIS WAY

My life began on the 1st of May, 1908, and between one thing and another, it still goes on.

When I was born my mother had been teaching in the elementary school for nine years and she continued to teach until the end of 1949. In recognition of her work the parish priest of the village presented her with an alarm clock in the name of all the people and after fifty years of teaching in schools where there was no electric light or water but, in compensation, an abundant supply of cockroaches, flies and mosquitos, my mother now passes her time waiting for the state to consider her request for a pension and listening to the tick-tock of the alarm clock given her by the village.

At the time when I was born my father was interested in all kinds of machines, from harvesters to gramophones and he possessed an enormous mustache, very similar to the one I wear under my nose. He still has the splendid mustache but for some time he has not been interested in much of anything and he passes his time reading the newspapers. He also reads what I write but he does not like my way of writing and thinking.

In his day my father was a very brilliant man and he traveled around by automobile at a time, in Italy, when entire populations went from one town to another in order to see that darned machine that ran by itself. The only memory I have of these ancient splendors is an old automobile horn—the kind with the rubber ball that you squeeze. My father screwed this to the head of his bed and he used to sound it every so often, especially in the summertime.

I also have a brother but I had an argument with him two weeks ago and I prefer not to discuss him.

In addition to the above I have a motorcycle with four cylinders, an automobile with six cylinders and a wife and two children.

My parents had decided that I should become a naval engineer and so I ended up studying law and thus, in a short time, I became famous as a signboard artist and caricaturist. Since no one at school had ever made me study drawing, drawing naturally had a particular fascination for me and, after doing caricatures and public advertisements, I studied wood-carving and scenic design.

At the same time I kept busy as a doorman in a sugar refinery, a superintendent of a parking lot for bicycles, and since I knew nothing at all about music I began to give mandolin lessons to some friends. I had an excellent record as a census taker. I was a teacher in a boarding school and then I got a job correcting proof on a local newspaper. To supplement my modest salary I began to write stories about local events and since I had a free day on Sunday I took over the editorship of the weekly magazine which came out on Monday. In order to get it together as quickly as possible I wrote three-quarters of it.

One fine day I took a train and went to Milan where I wormed my way into a humor magazine called *Bertoldo.* Here I was forced to stop writing but I was allowed to draw. I took advantage of this by drawing in white on black paper, something which created vast depressed areas in the magazine.

I was born in Parma near the Po River; people born in this area have heads hard as pig iron and I succeeded in becoming editor-in-chief of *Bertoldo.* This is the magazine in which Saul Steinberg, who at that time was studying architecture in Milan, published his first drawings and for which he worked until he left to go to America.

For reasons entirely beyond my control the war broke out and one day in 1942 I went on a terrific drunk because my brother was lost in Russia and I couldn't find out anything about him. That night I went up and down the streets of Milan shouting things which filled several sheets of legal-size paper—as I found out the next day when I was arrested by the political police. Then a lot of people worried about me and they finally got me released. However, the political police wanted me out of circulation and so had me called into the army, and on the 9th of September, 1943, with the fall of Fascism I was taken prisoner again, this time at Alessandria in Northern Italy by the Germans. Since I did not want to work for the Germans I was sent to a Polish concentration camp. I was in various German concentration camps until April, 1945, when my camp was taken over by the English and after five months I was sent back to Italy.

The period I spent in prison was the most intensely active of my life. In fact I had to do everything to stay alive and succeeded almost completely by dedicating myself to a precise program which is summarized in my slogan, "I will not die even if they kill me." (It is not easy to remain alive when one is reduced to a sack of bones of which the total weight is one hundred pounds and this includes lice, bedbugs, fleas, hunger and melancholy.)

When I returned to Italy I found that many things were changed, especially the Italians, and I spent a good deal of time trying to figure out whether they had changed for the better or for the worse. In the end I discovered that they had not changed at all and then I became so depressed that I shut myself in my house.

Shortly thereafter a new magazine called *Candido* was established in Milan and, in working for it, I found myself up to my eyes in politics although I was then, and still am, an independent. Nevertheless the magazine values my contributions very highly—perhaps because I am editor-in-chief.

A few months ago the leader of the Italian Communists, Mr. Palmiro Togliatti, made a speech in which he lost his temper and called the Milanese journalist who invented the character with the triple nostrils "a triple idiot." The three-fold idiot is me and this was for me the most prized recognition of my work as a political journalist. The man with three nostrils is now famous in Italy and it was I who created him. I must admit that I am proud because to succeed in characterizing a Communist with a stroke of the pen (that is, putting under the nose three, instead of two, nostrils) is not a bad idea and it worked very well.

And why should I be modest? The other things that I wrote and drew during the days before the election also worked very well; to prove it I have in my attic a sack full of newspaper clippings which malign me; whoever wants to know more can come and read them.

The stories in *The Little World of Don Camillo* were very successful in Italy and this book, which collects the first series of these stories, is already in its seventh edition. Many people have written long articles on *The Little World of Don Camillo* and many people have written me letters about this or that story, and so now I am a little confused and I would find myself rather embarrassed if I had to make any judgment of *The Little World of Don Camillo.* The background of these stories is my home, Parma, the Emilian Plain along the Po where political passion often reaches a disturbing intensity, and yet these people are attractive and hospitable and generous and have a highly developed sense of humor. It must be the sun, a terrible sun which beats on their brains during the summer, or perhaps it is the fog, a heavy fog which oppresses them during the winter.

The people in these stories are true to life and the stories are so true that more than once, after I had written a story, the thing actually happened and one read it in the news.

In fact the truth surpasses the imagination. I once wrote a story about the Communist, Peppone, who was annoyed during a political meeting by an airplane which threw down pamphlets of the opposition. Peppone took up a machine gun but he could not bring himself to fire on the plane. When I wrote this I said to myself, "This is too fantastic." Some months later at Spilimberg not only did the Communists fire on an airplane that distributed anti-Communist pamphlets but they shot it down.

I have nothing more to say about *The Little World of Don Camillo.* You can't expect that after a poor fellow has written a book he should also understand it.

I am 5'10" high and have written eight books in all. I have also done a movie which is called *People Like This,* now being distributed throughout Italy. Many people like the movie, others do not like it. As far as I am concerned the movie leaves me indifferent. Many things in life leave me indifferent now but that is not my fault. It is the fault of the war. The war destroyed a lot of things we had within us. We have seen too many dead and too many living. In addition to 5'10" I have all my hair.

THE LITTLE WORLD

The Little World of Don Camillo is to be found somewhere in the valley of the Po River. It is almost any village on that stretch of plain in Northern Italy. There, between the Po and the Apennines, the climate is always the same. The landscape never changes and, in country like this, you can stop along any road for a moment and look at a farmhouse sitting in the midst of maize and hemp—and immediately a story is born.

Why do I tell you this instead of getting on with my story? Because I want you to understand that, in the Little World between the river and the mountains, many things can happen that cannot happen anywhere else. Here, the deep, eternal breathing of the river freshens the air, for both the living and the dead, and even the dogs, have souls. If you keep this in mind, you will easily come to know the village priest, Don Camillo, and his adversary Peppone, the Communist Mayor. You will not be surprised that Christ watches the goings-on from a big cross in the village church and not infrequently talks, and that one man beats the other over the head, but fairly—that is, without hatred—and that in the end the two enemies find they agree about essentials.

And one final word of explanation before I begin my story. If there is a priest anywhere who feels offended by my treatment of Don Camillo, he is welcome to break the biggest candle available over my head. And if there is a Communist who feels offended by Peppone, he is welcome to break a hammer and sickle on my back. But if there is anyone who is offended by the conversations of Christ, I can't help it; for the one who speaks in this story is not Christ but my Christ—that is, the voice of my conscience.

A CONFESSION

Don Camillo had come into the world with a constitutional preference for calling a spade a spade. His parishioners remembered the time he found out about a local scandal involving young girls of the village with some landowners well along in years. On the Sunday following his discovery, Don Camillo had begun a simple, rather mild sermon, when he spotted one of the offenders in the front pew. Taking just enough time out to throw a cloth over the crucifix at the main altar so that Christ might not hear what was going to follow, he turned on the congregation with clenched fists and finished the sermon in a voice so loud and with words so strong that the roof of the little church trembled.

Naturally, when the time of the elections drew near, Don Camillo was very explicit in his allusions to the local leftists. What happened was not surprising, therefore: one fine evening as the priest was on his way home, a fellow muffled in a cloak sprang out of a hedge and, taking advantage of the fact that Don Camillo was handicapped by a bicycle with a basket of eggs on the handlebars, dealt the priest a mean blow with a heavy stick and then disappeared, as if the earth had swallowed him.

Don Camillo kept his own council. He continued to the rectory and, after putting the eggs in a safe place, went into the church to talk things over with Christ, as he always did in moments of perplexity.

"What should I do?" asked Don Camillo.

"Anoint your back with a little oil beaten up in water and hold your tongue," Christ answered from the main altar. "We must forgive those who offend us."

"Very true, Lord, but here we are discussing blows, not offenses."

"And what do you mean by that? Surely, Don Camillo, you don't mean that the injuries done to the body are more painful than those to the soul?"

"I see Your point, Lord. But You should bear in mind that an attack on me, Your priest, is also an offense against You. I am really more concerned for You than for myself."

"And wasn't I a greater minister of God than you are? And didn't I forgive those who nailed Me to the cross?"

"There's no use arguing with You!" Don Camillo exclaimed. "You are always right. May Your will be done. I will forgive, but don't forget that if these ruffians, encouraged by my silence, crack my skull open, it will be Your responsibility. I could quote You several passages from the Old Testament . . ."

"Don Camillo, do you propose to teach Me the Old Testament! As for this business, I assume full responsibility. And just between ourselves, that little beating this evening did you some good. It may teach you to let politics alone in My house."

Don Camillo forgave in his heart, but one thing stuck in his mind and needled him—curiosity as to the identity of his assailant.

Time passed. Then, late one evening as he was sitting in the confessional, Don Camillo recognized through the grille the face of Peppone, the leader of the extreme left.

That Peppone should come to confession at all was a sensational event, and Don Camillo was duly gratified.

"God be with you, brother; with you who, more than others, needs his Holy blessing. When did you make your last confession?"

"In 1918," replied Peppone.

"In all those years you must have committed a lot of sins with your head so crammed with crazy ideas . . ."

"Quite a few, I'm afraid," sighed Peppone.

"For example?"

"For example, two months ago I gave you a beating."

"That is very serious," replied Don Camillo, "since, by assaulting one of God's priests, you have offended God Himself."

"Oh, but I have repented," Peppone exclaimed. "And anyway it was not as God's priest that I beat you up but as my political adversary. Anyhow I did it in a moment of weakness."

"Besides this and your activities in that devilish party, have you any other sins to confess?"

Peppone spilled them out, but all in all Don Camillo found nothing very serious and let him off with twenty Our Fathers and twenty Hail Marys. While Peppone was at the altar rail saying his penance, Don Camillo went and knelt before the crucifix.

"Lord," he said, "forgive me but I'm going to beat him up for You."

"You'll do nothing of the kind," replied Christ. "I have forgiven him and you must do the same. After all, he's not such a bad soul."

"Lord, you can't trust a red! They live by lies. Just look at that face —Barabbas incarnate!"

"One face is the same as another. It's your heart, Don Camillo, that is venomous!"

"Lord, if I have been a worthy servant to You, grant me one small favor. Let me at least hit him with this candle. After all, Lord, what is a candle?"

"No," replied Christ. "Your hands were made for blessing."

Don Camillo sighed wearily. He genuflected and left the altar. As he turned to make a final sign of the cross, he found himself exactly behind Peppone, who still knelt at the altar rail and appeared absorbed in prayer.

"Lord," groaned Don Camillo, clasping his hands and looking up at the crucifix, "my hands were made for blessing, but not my feet."

"There's something in that," replied Christ, "but, I warn you, just one."

The kick landed like a thunderbolt. Peppone didn't bat an eye. After a minute he got up and sighed.

"I've been expecting that for the past ten minutes," he remarked casually. "I feel better now."

"So do I," exclaimed Don Camillo whose heart was now as light and serene as a May morning.

Christ said nothing at all, but it was easy enough to see that He too was pleased.

A BAPTISM

One day Don Camillo, perched high on a ladder, was busily polishing St. Joseph's halo. Unexpectedly a man and two women, one of whom was Peppone's wife, came into the church. Don Camillo turned around to ask what they wanted.

"There is something here to be baptized," replied the man, and one of the women held up a bundle containing a baby.

"Whose is it?" inquired Don Camillo, coming down from his ladder.

"Mine," replied Peppone's wife.

"And your husband's?" persisted Don Camillo.

"Well, naturally! Who else would be the father? You, maybe?" retorted Peppone's wife indignantly.

"No need to be offended," observed Don Camillo on his way to the sacristy. "I've been told often enough that your party approves of free love."

As he passed before the high altar Don Camillo knelt down and gave a discreet wink in the direction of Christ. "Did you hear that one?" he murmured with a happy grin. "One in the eye for the Godless ones!"

"Don't talk rubbish, Don Camillo," replied Christ irritably. "If they had no God why should they come here to get their child baptized? If Peppone's wife had boxed your ears it would have served you right."

"If Peppone's wife had boxed my ears I should have taken the three of them by the scruff of their necks and . . ."

"And what?" Christ asked severely.

"Oh, nothing; just a figure of speech," Don Camillo hastened to assure Him, rising to his feet.

"Don Camillo, watch your step," Christ said sternly.

Duly vested, Don Camillo approached the baptismal font. "What do you wish to name this child?" he asked Peppone's wife.

"Lenin, Libero, Antonio," she replied.

"Then go and get him baptized in Russia," said Don Camillo calmly, replacing the cover on the font.

The priest's hands were as big as shovels and the three left the church without protest. But as Don Camillo tried to slip into the sacristy he was stopped by the voice of Christ. "Don Camillo, you have done a very wicked thing. Go at once and bring those people back and baptize their child."

"But, Lord," protested Don Camillo, "You really must bear in mind that baptism is a very sacred matter. Baptism is . . ."

"Don Camillo," Christ interrupted him, "are you trying to teach Me the nature of baptism? Didn't I invent it? I tell you that you have been guilty of gross presumption, because if that child were to die at this moment it would be your fault if it failed to attain Paradise!"

"Lord, let us not be melodramatic! Why in the name of Heaven should it die? It's as pink and white as a rose!"

"That doesn't mean a thing!" Christ pointed out. "What if a tile should fall on its head or it suddenly had convulsions? It was your duty to baptize it."

Don Camillo raised his hands in protest. "But, Lord, think it over. If it were certain that the child would go to Hell, then we might stretch a point. But since he might easily manage to slip into Heaven, in spite of his father, how can You ask me to risk anyone getting in there with a name like Lenin? I'm thinking of the reputation of Heaven."

"The reputation of Heaven is My business," shouted Christ angrily. "What matters to Me is that a man should be a decent fellow, and I care less than nothing whether his name be Lenin or Button. At the very most, you should have pointed out to those people that saddling children with fantastic names may be a nuisance to them when they grow up."

"Very well," replied Don Camillo. "I am always wrong. I'll see what I can do."

Just then someone came into the church. It was Peppone, alone, with the baby in his arms. He closed the church door behind him and bolted it. "I'm not leaving this church," he said, "until my son has been baptized with the name that I have chosen."

"Look at that," whispered Don Camillo, smiling as he turned to Christ. "Now do You see what these people are? One is filled with the holiest intentions, and this is how they treat You."

"Put yourself in his place," Christ replied. "One may not approve of his attitude but one can understand it."

Don Camillo shook his head.

"I have already said that I do not leave this place unless you baptize my son!" repeated Peppone. After laying the bundle containing the baby upon a bench, he took off his coat, rolled up his sleeves, and came toward the priest threateningly.

"Lord," implored Don Camillo. "I ask You! If You think one of Your priests should give way to the threats of a layman, then I must obey. But if I do and tomorrow they bring me a calf and compel me to baptize it, You must not complain. You know very well how dangerous it is to create precedents."

"All right, but in this case you must try to make him understand . . ."

"And if he hits me?"

"Then you must accept it. You must endure and suffer as I did."

Don Camillo turned to his visitor. "Very well, Peppone," he said. "The baby will leave the church baptized, but not with that accursed name."

"Don Camillo," stuttered Peppone, "don't forget that my stomach has never recovered from that bullet I stopped in the mountains. If you hit low I go after you with a bench."

"Don't worry, Peppone; I can deal with you entirely in the upper stories," Don Camillo assured him, landing a quick one above his ear.

They were both burly men and their blows whistled through the air. After twenty minutes of speechless and furious combat, Don Camillo distinctly heard a voice behind him.

"Now, Don Camillo! A left to the jaw!" It came from Christ above the altar. Don Camillo struck hard and Peppone crashed to the ground.

He remained there for about ten minutes; then he sat up, got to his feet, rubbed his jaw, shook himself, put on his jacket and re-knotted his red handkerchief. Then he picked up the baby. Fully vested, Don Camillo was waiting, steady as a rock, beside the font. Peppone approached him slowly.

"What are we going to name him?" asked Don Camillo.

"Camillo, Libero, Antonio," muttered Peppone.

Don Camillo shook his head. "No; we will name him Libero, Camillo, Lenin," he said. "After all, the Camillo will cancel out Lenin any day."

"Amen," muttered Peppone, still massaging his jaw.

When all was done and Don Camillo passed before the altar, Christ smiled and remarked: "Don Camillo, I have to admit that in politics you are My master."

"And in boxing," replied Don Camillo with perfect gravity, carelessly fingering a large lump on his forehead.

ON THE TRAIL

Don Camillo had let himself go a bit in the course of a little sermon. He had made some rather pointed allusions to *"certain people,"* and so on the following evening when he seized the ropes of the church bells all hell broke loose. Some damned soul had tied firecrackers to the clappers of the bells. No harm done of course, but there was a din of explosions shattering enough to give the ringer heart failure.

Don Camillo said nothing. He celebrated the evening service in perfect composure before a crowded congregation. Peppone was in the front row, and every countenance was a picture of fervor. It was enough to infuriate a saint, but Don Camillo was no novice in self-control and his audience went home disappointed.

As soon as the big doors of the church were closed, Don Camillo snatched up an overcoat and on his way out made a hasty genuflection before the altar.

"Don Camillo," said Christ, "put it down."

"I don't understand," protested Don Camillo.

"Put it down!"

Don Camillo drew a heavy stick out from under his coat and laid it in front of the altar.

"Not a pleasant sight, Don Camillo."

"But, Lord! It isn't even oak; it's only poplar, light and supple," Don Camillo pleaded.

"Go to bed, Don Camillo, and forget about Peppone."

Don Camillo threw up his hands and went to bed with a temperature. But on the following evening when Peppone's wife came to the rectory, he leaped to his feet as though a firecracker had gone off under his chair.

"Don Camillo," began the woman, who was obviously upset. But Don Camillo interrupted her.

"Get out of my sight, sacrilegious creature!"

"Don Camillo, never mind about that foolishness. At Castellino there is that poor devil who tried to support Peppone. They have driven him out of the village!"

Don Camillo counted to ten and lit a cigar. "Well, what of it, comrade? Why should you bother about it?"

The woman started to shout. "I'm bothering because they came to tell Peppone, and he has gone rushing off to Castellino like a lunatic. And he has taken his Tommy gun with him!"

"I see; then you have got concealed arms, have you?"

"Don Camillo, never mind about politics! Can't you understand that Peppone is out to kill? Unless you help me, my husband is done for!"

Don Camillo laughed unpleasantly. "Which will teach him to tie firecrackers to my bells. I shall be pleased to watch him die in jail! You get out of my house!"

Ten minutes later, Don Camillo, with his skirts tucked up almost to his neck, was pedaling like a lunatic along the road to Castellino on a racing bike that belonged to the son of his assistant.

There was a splendid moon and when he was within a few miles of Castellino, Don Camillo saw by its light a man sitting on the wall of the little bridge that spans the river. He slowed down, since it is always best to be prudent when one travels by night, and stopped some ten yards from the bridge, holding in his hand a small object that he happened to have had in his pocket.

"Have you seen a big man go by on a bicycle in the direction of Castellino?" he asked.

"No, Don Camillo," replied the other quietly.

Don Camillo drew nearer. "Have you already been to Castellino?"

"No. I thought it over. It wasn't worthwhile. Was it my fool of a wife who put you to this trouble?"

"Trouble? Nothing of the kind . . . a little constitutional!"

"Have you any idea what a priest looks like on a racing bicycle?" snickered Peppone.

Don Camillo came and sat beside him on his wall. "My son, you must be prepared to see all kinds of things in this world."

Less than an hour later, Don Camillo was back at the rectory and went to report to Christ.

"Everything went according to Your commandments."

"Well done, Don Camillo; but would you mind telling Me who commanded you to grab him by the feet and tumble him into the ditch?"

Don Camillo raised his arms. "To tell You the truth, I can't remember exactly. As a matter of fact he seemed to find the sight of a priest on a racing bike distasteful, so I thought it only kind to stop him from seeing it any longer."

"I understand. Has he got back yet?"

"He'll be here soon. It struck me that in his rather damp condition, he might find the bicycle in his way, so I thought it best to bring it along with me."

"Very kind of you, I'm sure, Don Camillo," said Christ with perfect gravity.

Just before dawn Peppone appeared at the door of the rectory. He was soaked to the skin, and Don Camillo asked if it was raining.

"Fog," replied Peppone with chattering teeth. "May I have my bicycle?"

"Why, of course. There it is."

"Are you sure there wasn't a Tommy gun tied to it?"

Don Camillo smiled. "A Tommy gun? And what is that?"

As he turned from the door Peppone said, "I have made one mistake in my life. I tied firecrackers to your bells. It should have been half a ton of dynamite."

"Errare humanum est," remarked Don Camillo.

NIGHT SCHOOL

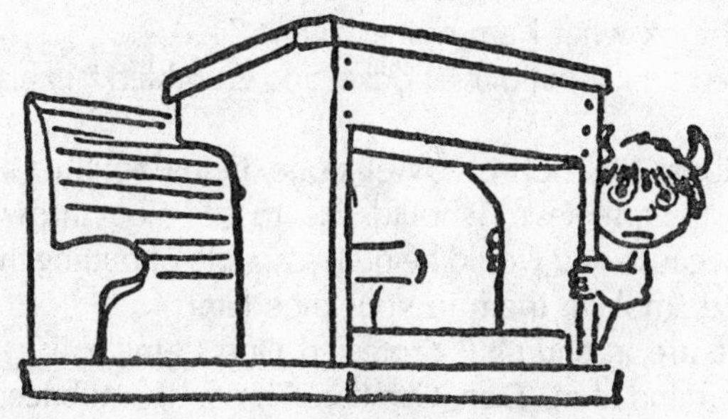

In the empty church by the faint light of the two altar candles, Don Camillo was chatting with Christ about the outcome of the local elections.

"I don't presume to criticize Your actions," he wound up, "but I would never have let Peppone become Mayor, with a Council in which only two people really know how to read and write properly."

"Culture is not important, Don Camillo," replied Christ with a smile. "What counts are ideas. Eloquent speeches get nowhere unless there are practical ideas at the back of them. Before judging, suppose we put them to the test."

"Fair enough," conceded Don Camillo. "I really said what I did because if the lawyer's party had come out on top, I had assurances that the bell tower of the church would be repaired. Now if it falls down, the people will have the compensation of watching the construction of a magnificent People's Palace for dancing, sale of alcoholic liquors, gambling and a theater."

"And a jail for venomous reptiles like Don Camillo," added Christ.

Don Camillo lowered his head. "Lord, You misjudge me," he said. "You know how much a cigar means to me? Well, look: this is my last cigar, and look what I am doing with it."

He pulled a cigar out of his pocket and crumbled it in his enormous hand.

"Well done," said Christ. "Well done, Don Camillo. I accept your penance. Nevertheless I should like to see you throw away the crumbs, because you would be quite capable of putting them in your pocket and smoking them in your pipe later."

"But we are in church," protested Don Camillo.

"Never mind that, Don Camillo. Throw the tobacco into that corner." Don Camillo obeyed while Christ looked on with approval, and just then a knocking was heard at the little door of the sacristy and Peppone came in.

"Good evening, Mr. Mayor," said Don Camillo with deference.

"Listen," said Peppone. "If a Christian were in doubt about something that he had done and came to tell you about it, and if you found that he had made some mistakes, would you point them out to him or would you simply leave him in ignorance?"

Don Camillo protested indignantly. "How can you dare to doubt the honesty of a priest? His primary duty is to point out clearly all the penitent sinner's mistakes."

"Very well, then," exclaimed Peppone. "Are you quite ready to hear my confession?"

"I'm ready."

Peppone pulled a large sheet of paper out of his pocket and began to read: "Citizens, at the moment when we are hailing the victorious affirmation of our party . . ."

Don Camillo interrupted him with a gesture and went to kneel before the altar. "Lord," he murmured, "I am no longer responsible for my actions."

"But I am," said Christ promptly. "Peppone has outsmarted you and you must play fair, and do your duty."

"But, Lord," persisted Don Camillo, "You realize, don't You, that You are making me work for the Party?"

"You are working in the interests of grammar, syntax and spelling, none of which is either diabolical or sectarian."

Don Camillo put on his glasses, grasped a pencil, and set to work correcting the speech that Peppone was to make the following day. Peppone read it through intently.

"Good," he approved. "There is only one thing that I do not understand. Where I had said: *'It is our intention to extend the schools and to rebuild the bridge over the Fossalto'* you have substituted: *'It is our intention to extend the schools, repair the church tower and rebuild the bridge over the Fossalto.'* Why is that?"

"Merely a question of syntax," explained Don Camillo gravely.

"Blessed are those who have studied Latin and who are able to understand niceties of language," sighed Peppone. "And so," he added, "we are to lose even the hope that the tower may collapse on your head!"

Don Camillo raised his arms. "We must all bow before the will of God!"

After seeing Peppone to the door, Don Camillo came to say good night to Christ.

"Well done, Don Camillo," said Christ with a smile. "I was unfair to you and I am sorry you destroyed your last cigar. It was a penance that you did not deserve. Nevertheless, we may as well be frank about it: Peppone was a skunk not to offer you even a cigar, after all the trouble you took!"

"Oh, all right," sighed Don Camillo, fishing a cigar from his pocket and preparing to crush it in his big hand.

"No, Don Camillo," smiled Christ. "Go and smoke it in peace. You have earned it."

"But . . ."

"No, Don Camillo; you didn't exactly steal it. Peppone had two cigars in his pocket. Peppone is a Communist. He believes in sharing things. By skillfully relieving him of one cigar, you only took your fair share."

"You always know best," exclaimed Don Camillo.

OUT OF BOUNDS

Don Camillo used to go back and measure the famous crack in the church tower, and every morning his inspection met with the same result: the crack got no wider but neither did it get smaller. Finally he lost his temper, and the day came when he sent the sacristan to the Town Hall.

"Go and tell the Mayor to come at once and look at this damage. Explain that the matter is serious."

The sacristan went and returned.

"Peppone says that he will take your word for it that it is a serious matter. He also said that if you really want to show him the crack, you had better take the tower to him in his office. He will be there until five o'clock."

Don Camillo didn't bat an eye; all he said was, "If Peppone or any member of his gang has the courage to turn up at Mass tomorrow morning, I'll fix them. But they know it and probably not one of them will come."

The next morning there was not a sign of a "red" in church, but five minutes before Mass was due to begin the sound of marching was heard outside the church. In perfect formation all the "reds," not only those of the village but also those of the neighboring cells, including the cobbler, Bilo, who had a wooden leg and Roldo dei Prati, who was shivering with fever, came marching proudly toward the church led by Peppone. They took their places in the church, sitting in a solid phalanx with faces as ferocious as Russian generals.

Don Camillo finished his sermon on the parable of the good Samaritan, with a brief plea to the faithful.

"As you all know, a most dangerous crack is threatening the church tower. I therefore appeal to you, my dear brethren, to come to the assistance of the house of God. In using the term 'brethren,' I am addressing those who came here with a desire to draw near to God, and not certain people who come only in order to parade their militarism. To such as these, it can matter nothing should the tower fall to the ground."

The Mass over, Don Camillo settled himself at a table near the door, and the congregation filed past him. Each one, after making the expected donation, joined the crowd in the little square in front of the church to watch developments. And last of all came Peppone, followed by his battalion in perfect formation. They drew to a defiant halt before the table.

Peppone stepped forward proudly.

"From this tower, in the past, the bells have hailed the dawn of freedom and from it, tomorrow, they shall welcome the glorious dawn of the proletarian revolution," Peppone said to Don Camillo, as he laid on the table three large red handkerchiefs full of money.

Then he turned on his heel and marched away, followed by his gang. And Roldo dei Prati was shaking with fever and could scarcely remain on his feet, but he held his head erect, and the crippled Bilo as he passed Don Camillo stamped his wooden leg defiantly in perfect step with his comrades.

When Don Camillo went to the Lord to show Him the basket containing the money and told Him that there was more than enough for the repair of the tower, Christ smiled in astonishment.

"I guess your sermon did the trick, Don Camillo."

"Naturally," replied Don Camillo. "You see, You understand humanity, but I know Italians."

Up to that point Don Camillo had behaved pretty well. But he made a mistake when he sent a message to Peppone saying that he admired the military smartness of the men but advising Peppone to give them more intensive drilling in the right-about-face and the double, which they would need badly on the day of the proletarian revolution.

This was deplorable and Peppone planned to retaliate.

Don Camillo was an honest man, but in addition to an overwhelming passion for hunting, he possessed a splendid double-barreled gun and a good supply of cartridges. Moreover, Baron Stocco's private preserve lay only three miles from the village. It presented a permanent temptation, because not only game but even the neighborhood poultry had learned that they were in safety behind the fence of wire netting.

It was therefore not astonishing that on a certain evening Don Camillo, his cassock bundled into an enormous pair of breeches and his face partly concealed beneath the brim of an old felt hat, should find himself actually on the business side of the Baron's fence. The flesh is weak and the flesh of the sportsman particularly so.

Nor was it surprising, since Don Camillo was a good shot, that he brought down a fine rabbit almost under his nose. He stuffed it into his game bag and was making a getaway when he suddenly came face to face with another trespasser. There was no alternative but to butt the stranger in the stomach with the hope of knocking him out and thereby saving the countryside the embarrassment of learning that their parish priest had been caught poaching.

Unfortunately, the stranger conceived the same idea at the same moment. The two heads met with a crack that left both men side by side on the ground seeing stars.

"A skull as hard as that can only belong to our beloved Mayor," muttered Don Camillo, as his vision began to clear.

"A skull as hard as that can only belong to our beloved priest," replied Peppone, scratching his head. For Peppone, too, was poaching on forbidden ground and he, too, had a fine rabbit in his game bag. His eyes gleamed as he observed Don Camillo.

"Never would I have believed that the very man who preaches respect for other people's property would be found breaking through the fences of a preserve to go poaching," said Peppone.

"Nor would I have believed that our chief citizen, our comrade Mayor——"

"Citizen, yes, but also comrade," Peppone interrupted, "and therefore perverted by those diabolical theories of the fair distribution of all property, and therefore acting more in accordance with his known views than the reverend Don Camillo, who, for his part . . ."

This ideological analysis was suddenly interrupted. Someone was approaching them and was so near that it was quite impossible to escape without the risk of stopping a bullet, for the intruder happened to be a gamekeeper.

"We've got to do something!" whispered Don Camillo. "Think of the scandal if we are recognized!"

"Personally, I don't care," replied Peppone with composure. "I am always ready to answer for my actions."

The steps drew nearer, and Don Camillo crouched against a large tree trunk. Peppone made no attempt to move, and when the gamekeeper appeared with his gun over his arm, Peppone greeted him:

"Good evening."

"What are you doing here?" inquired the gamekeeper.

"Looking for mushrooms."

"With a gun?"

"As good a way as another."

The means whereby a gamekeeper can be rendered innocuous are fairly simple. If one happens to be standing behind him, it suffices to muffle his head unexpectedly in an overcoat and give him a good crack on the head. Then advantage can be taken of his momentary unconsciousness to reach the fence and scramble over it. Once over, all is well.

Don Camillo and Peppone found themselves sitting behind a bush a good mile away from the Baron's estate.

"Don Camillo!" sighed Peppone. "We have committed a serious offense. We have raised our hands against one in authority!"

Don Camillo, who had actually been the one to raise them, broke out into a cold sweat.

"My conscience troubles me," continued Peppone, watching his companion closely. "I shall have no peace. How can I go before a priest of God to ask forgiveness for such a misdeed? It was an evil day when I listened to the infamous 'Muscovite doctrine,' forgetting the holy precepts of Christian charity!"

Don Camillo was so deeply humiliated that he wanted to cry. On the other hand, he also wanted to land one good crack on the skull of his perverted adversary. As Peppone was well aware of this, he stopped talking for the moment. Then suddenly he shouted, "Accursed temptation!" and pulled the rabbit out of his bag and threw it on the ground.

"Accursed indeed!" shouted Don Camillo, and hauling out his own rabbit he flung it far into the snow and walked away with bent head. Peppone followed him as far as the crossroad and then turned to the right.

"By the way," he said, pausing for a moment, "could you tell me of a reputable parish priest in this neighborhood to whom I could go and confess this sin?"

Don Camillo clenched his fists and walked straight ahead.

When he had gathered sufficient courage, Don Camillo went before the main altar of the church. "I didn't do it to save myself, Lord," he said. "I did it simply because, if it were known that I go poaching, the Church would have been the chief sufferer from the scandal."

But Christ remained silent. Now whenever this happened Don Camillo acquired a fever and put himself on a diet of bread and water for days and days, until Christ felt sorry for him and said: "Enough."

This time, Christ said nothing until the bread and water diet had continued for seven days. Don Camillo was so weak that he could remain standing only by leaning against a wall, and his stomach was rumbling from hunger.

Then Peppone came to confession.

"I have sinned against the law and against Christian charity," said Peppone.

"I know it," replied Don Camillo.

"What you don't know is that, as soon as you were out of sight, I went back and collected both the rabbits. I have roasted one and stewed the other."

"Just what I supposed you would do," murmured Don Camillo. And when he passed the altar a little later, Christ smiled at him, not so much because of the prolonged fast as because Don Camillo, when he murmured "Just what I supposed you would do," had felt no desire to hit Peppone. Instead he had felt profound shame, recalling that on that same evening he himself had had a momentary temptation to do exactly the same thing.

"Poor Don Camillo," whispered Christ tenderly. And Don Camillo spread out his arms as though he wished to say that he did his best and that if he sometimes made mistakes it was not deliberately.

"I know, I know, Don Camillo," replied the Lord. "And now get along and eat your rabbit—for Peppone has left it for you, nicely cooked, in your kitchen."

THE TREASURE

One day Smilzo came to the rectory. He was a young ex-partisan who had been Peppone's orderly during the fighting in the mountains and now worked as a messenger at the Town Hall. He was the bearer of a handsome letter, printed on handmade paper with the Party heading in Gothic lettering, which read:

"Your honor is invited to grace with his presence a ceremony of a social nature which will take place tomorrow at ten o'clock A.M. *in the Plaza of Liberty. The Secretary of the Section, Comrade Bottazzi, Mayor, Giuseppe."*

Don Camillo looked severely at Smilzo. "Tell Comrade Peppone Mayor Giuseppe that I have no wish to go and listen to the usual imbecilities against reaction and the capitalists. I already know them by heart."

"No," explained Smilzo, "there won't be any political speeches. This is for patriotism and social activities. If you refuse, it means that you don't understand democracy."

Don Camillo nodded his head slowly. "If that's it," he said, "then I have nothing more to say."

"Good. And the Mayor says you are to come in uniform and to bring all your paraphernalia."

"Paraphernalia?"

"Yes—a pail of holy water and all that stuff; there is something to be blessed."

Smilzo got away with talking this way to Don Camillo precisely because he was Smilzo, that is, the lean one. He was so skinny and quick that during the fighting in the mountains he had been known to slip between the bullets. Therefore, by the time the heavy book Don Camillo hurled at him reached the spot where his head had been, Smilzo was already on his bike pedaling away for all he was worth.

Don Camillo got up, rescued the book and went to the church to let off steam. When he reached the altar he said, "Lord, I must find out what those people are planning to do tomorrow. I never heard of anything so mysterious. What is the meaning of all those preparations? All those branches that they are sticking into the ground round the meadow between the drugstore and Baghetti's house? What kind of deviltry can they be up to?"

"My son, if it were deviltry, first of all they wouldn't be doing it in the open and secondly they wouldn't be sending for you to bless it. Be patient until tomorrow."

That evening Don Camillo went to have a look around but saw nothing but branches and decorations surrounding the meadow, and nobody seemed to know anything.

When he set out next morning, followed by two acolytes, his knees were trembling. He felt that something was not as it should be, that there was treachery in the air.

An hour later he returned, shattered and with a temperature.

"What happened?" asked Christ from the altar.

"Enough to make one's hair stand on end," stammered Don Camillo. "A terrible thing. A band, Garibaldi's hymn, a speech from Peppone, and the laying of the first stone of 'The People's Palace'! And I had to bless the stone while Peppone chuckled with joy. And the ruffian asked me to say a few words, and I had to make a suitable little address because, although it is a Party affair, that dog dressed it up as a social undertaking."

Don Camillo paced back and forth in the empty church. Then he came to a standstill in front of Christ. "A mere trifle," he exclaimed. "An assembly hall, reading room, library, gymnasium, dispensary, and theater. A skyscraper of two floors with ground for sports and bowling. And the whole lot for the miserable sum of ten million lire."

"Not bad, given the high cost of building today," observed Christ.

Don Camillo sank down in a pew. "Lord," he moaned, "why have You done this to me?"

"Don Camillo, you are unreasonable."

"No, I'm not unreasonable. For ten years I have been praying to You on my knees to find me a little money so that I could build a library, an assembly hall for the young people, a playground for the children with a merry-go-round and swings and possibly a little swimming pool. For ten years I have humbled myself to bloated landowners when I would have preferred smacking them between the eyes every time I saw them. I must have organized two hundred bazaars and knocked at easily two thousand doors and I have nothing at all to show for it. Then this excommunicate dog comes along, and behold ten million lire drop into his pockets from Heaven."

Christ shook His head. "They didn't fall from Heaven," He replied. "He found them underground. I had nothing to do with it, Don Camillo. It is entirely due to his own personal initiative."

Don Camillo spread out his arms. "Then the obvious deduction is that I am a poor fool."

He went off to stamp up and down his study in the rectory, roaring with fury. He had to exclude the possibility that Peppone had got those ten million by holding people up on the roads or by robbing a bank.

He thought of the days of the liberation when Peppone came down from the mountains and it seemed as if the proletarian revolution might break out at any moment. "Peppone must have threatened those cowards of gentry and squeezed their money out of them," he said to himself. Then he remembered that in those days there had been no landowners in the neighborhood, but that there had been a detachment of the British Army which arrived simultaneously with Peppone and his men. The British moved into the landowners' houses, replacing the Germans who had stripped them of everything of any value. Therefore, Peppone couldn't have got the ten million by looting.

Maybe the money came from Russia? He burst out laughing; was it likely that the Russians should give a thought to Peppone?

At last he returned to the church. "Lord," he begged, from the foot of the altar, "won't You tell me where Peppone found the money?"

"Don Camillo," replied Christ with a smile, "do you take Me for a private detective? Why ask God to tell you the truth, when you have only to seek it within yourself? Look for it, Don Camillo, and meanwhile, in order to distract your mind, why not make a trip to the city?"

The following evening, when he got back from his excursion to the city, Don Camillo went before Christ in a condition of extreme agitation.

"What has upset you, Don Camillo?"

"Something quite mad," exclaimed Don Camillo breathlessly. "I have met a dead man! Face to face in the street!"

"Don Camillo, calm yourself and reflect. Usually the dead whom one meets face to face in the street are alive."

"This one cannot be!" shouted Don Camillo. "This one is as dead as mutton, and I know it because I myself carried him to the cemetery."

"If that is the case," Christ replied, "then I have nothing more to say. You must have seen a ghost."

Don Camillo shrugged his shoulders. "Of course not! Ghosts don't exist except in the minds of hysterical women!"

"And therefore?"

"Well . . ." muttered Don Camillo.

Don Camillo collected his thoughts. The deceased had been a thin young man who lived in a nearby village, and Don Camillo had seen him from time to time before the war. He had come down from the mountains with Peppone and his men and had been wounded in the head. Peppone put him up in the house which had been the German headquarters and which that day became the headquarters of the British Command. Peppone had his office in the room next to the invalid. Don Camillo remembered it all clearly: the villa was surrounded by sentries three deep and not a fly could leave it, because the British were still fighting nearby and were particularly careful of their own skins.

All this had happened one morning, and on the same evening the young man died. Peppone sent for Don Camillo toward midnight, but by the time he got there the young man was already in his coffin. The British didn't want the body in the house and so, at about noon, Peppone and his most trusted men carried out the coffin, covered with the Italian flag. A detachment of British soldiers had kindly volunteered to supply military honors.

Don Camillo recalled that the ceremony had been most moving. The whole village had walked behind the coffin which had been placed on a gun carriage. He himself had officiated, and his sermon before the body was lowered into the grave had people actually weeping. Peppone in the front row had sobbed.

"I certainly know how to express myself, when I put my mind to it!" said Don Camillo to himself complacently, recalling the episode. Then he took up his train of thought. "And in spite of all that, I could swear that the young man I met today in the city was the same one I followed to the grave."

He sighed. "Such is life!"

The following day, Don Camillo paid a visit to Peppone at his workshop where he found him lying on his back underneath a car.

"Good morning, Comrade Mayor. I want to tell you that for the past two days I have been thinking over your description of your 'People's Palace'!"

"And what do you think of it?" jeered Peppone.

"Magnificent! It has made me decide to start work on that scheme of a little place with a bathing-pool, garden, sports ground, theater, et cetera, which, as you know, I have planned for the past ten years. I expect to lay the foundation stone next Sunday. It would give me great pleasure if you, as Mayor, would attend the ceremony."

"Willingly—courtesy for courtesy."

"Meanwhile, you might try to trim down the plans for your own place a bit. It looks too big for my taste."

Peppone stared at him in amazement. "Don Camillo, are you crazy?"

"No more than when I conducted a funeral and made a patriotic address over a coffin that can't have been securely closed, because only yesterday I met the corpse walking about in the city."

Peppone sneered, "What are you trying to insinuate?"

"Nothing. Merely that the coffin to which the British presented arms was full of what you found in the cellars of that villa where the German Command had hidden it. And that the dead man was alive and hidden in the attic."

"A-a-h!" howled Peppone. "The same old story! An attempt to malign the partisan movement!"

"Leave the partisans out of it. They don't interest me!"

And he walked away while Peppone stood muttering vague threats.

That same evening, Don Camillo was reading the paper and waiting for Peppone. He arrived accompanied by Brusco and two other prominent supporters—the same men who had acted as pallbearers.

"You," said Peppone, "can drop your insinuations. It was all of it stuff looted by the Germans: silver, cameras, instruments, gold, et cetera. If we hadn't taken it, the British would have. We took the only possible means of getting it out of the place. I have witnesses and receipts: nobody has touched so much as a lira. Ten million was taken and ten million will be spent for the people."

Brusco, who was hot tempered, began to shout that it was God's truth and that he, if necessary, knew well enough how to deal with certain people.

"So do I," Don Camillo replied calmly. He dropped the newspaper which he had been holding in front of him, and it was easy to see that under his right armpit he held the famous Tommy gun that once belonged to Peppone.

Brusco turned pale but Peppone held up his hands. "Don Camillo —there is no need to quarrel."

"I agree," replied Don Camillo. "In fact, I agree all the way around. Ten million was acquired and ten million will be spent for the people. Seven on your People's Palace and three on my Recreation

Center for the people's children. *Suffer little children to come unto Me.* I ask only what is my due."

The four consulted together for a moment in undertones. Then Peppone spoke: "If you didn't have that damnable thing in your hands, I'd tell you that your suggestion is the filthiest blackmail in the world."

On the following Sunday, Peppone, together with all the village Council, assisted at the laying of the first stone of Don Camillo's Recreation Center. Peppone also made a short speech. However, he was able to whisper in Don Camillo's ear:

"It might be better to tie this stone around your neck and throw you in the Po."

That evening, Don Camillo went to report to Christ. "Well, what do You think about it?" he said after he had described the events of the day.

"Exactly what Peppone said. That if you didn't have that damnable thing in your hands, I should say that it was the filthiest blackmail in the world."

"But I have nothing at all in my hands except the check that Peppone has just given me."

"Precisely," whispered Christ. "And with that three million you are going to do so many beautiful things, Don Camillo, that I haven't the heart to scold you."

Don Camillo genuflected and went off to bed to dream of a garden full of children—a garden with a merry-go-round and a swing, and on the swing sat Peppone's youngest son, Libero Camillo Lenin, chirping joyfully like a fledgling.

RIVALRY

A big shot from the city was going to visit the village, and people were coming from all the surrounding cells. Therefore, Peppone decreed that the ceremony was to be held in the big square. He had a large platform decorated with red erected and got one of those trucks with four great loudspeakers and all the electric mechanism inside it for amplifying the voice.

And so, on the afternoon of that Sunday, the public square was crammed with people and so also was the church square, which happened to be next to it. Don Camillo shut all the doors and withdrew into the sacristy, so as to avoid seeing or hearing anything which would put him in a temper. He was actually dozing when a voice like the wrath of God roused him with a jerk as it bellowed: *"COMRADES! . . ."*

It was as though the walls had melted away.

Don Camillo went to work off his indignation at the high altar. "They must have aimed one of their accursed loudspeakers directly at the church," he exclaimed. "It is nothing short of violation of domicile."

"What can you do about it, Don Camillo? It is progress," replied Christ.

After a few generalizations, the voice got down to business and, since the speaker was an extremist, he made no bones about it. *"We must remain within the law and we shall do so! Even at the cost of taking up our weapons and using the firing squad on all the enemies of the people! . . ."*

Don Camillo was pawing the ground like a restive horse. "Lord, only listen to him!"

"I hear him, Don Camillo. I hear him only too well."

"Lord, why don't You drop a thunderbolt on all that rabble?"

"Don Camillo, let us remain within the law. If your method of driving the truth into the head of one who is in error is to shoot him down, what was the use of My crucifixion?"

Don Camillo shrugged. "You are right, of course. We can do nothing but wait for them to crucify us too."

Christ smiled. "If instead of speaking first and then thinking over what you have said, you thought first and did the speaking afterwards, you might not have to regret the foolish things you say."

Don Camillo bowed his head.

". . . as for those who, hiding in the shadow of the crucifix, attempt with the poison of their ambiguous words to spread dissension among the masses of the workers . . ." The voice of the loudspeaker, borne on the wind, filled the church and shook the bright-colored glass in the Gothic windows. Don Camillo grabbed a heavy bronze candlestick and, brandishing it like a club, made for the church door.

"Don Camillo, stop! You will not leave the church until everyone has gone away."

"Oh, very well," replied Don Camillo, putting the candlestick back on the altar. "I obey." He marched up and down the church and finally stopped in front of Christ. "But in here I can do as I please?"

"Naturally, Don Camillo. Here you are in your own house and free to do exactly as you wish. Short of climbing up to a window and firing at the people below."

Three minutes later, Don Camillo, leaping and bounding cheerfully in the bell chamber of the church tower, was performing the most infernal carillon that had ever been heard in the village.

The orator was forced to interrupt his speech and turned to the local authorities who were standing with him on the platform. "He must be stopped!" the big shot cried indignantly.

Peppone agreed gravely, nodding his head. "He must indeed," he replied, "and there are just two ways of stopping him. One is to explode a mine under the church tower and the other is to bombard it with heavy artillery."

The orator told him to stop talking nonsense. Surely it was easy enough to break in the door of the tower and climb the stairs.

"Well," said Peppone calmly, "you go up by ladders from landing to landing. Look, comrade, do you see those projections just by the big window of the belfry? They are the steps that the bellringer has removed as he went up. By closing the trap door of the top landing, he is cut off from the world."

"We might try firing at the windows of the tower!" suggested Smilzo.

"Certainly," agreed Peppone, "but we would have to knock him out with the first shot, otherwise he'd begin firing and then there might be trouble."

The bells stopped ringing for a moment, and the orator resumed his speech; all went well so long as he was careful to say nothing of which Don Camillo disapproved. Otherwise, Don Camillo immediately began a counterargument with his bells. In the end, the speech was merely pathetic and patriotic and was therefore respected by the threatening bells.

That evening, Peppone met Don Camillo. "Watch out, Don Camillo. This baiting could bring you to a bad end."

"There is no baiting involved," replied Don Camillo calmly. "You blow your trumpets and we ring our bells. That, comrade, is democracy. If on the other hand, only one person is allowed to perform, that is a dictatorship."

Peppone held his peace, but one morning Don Camillo got up to find a merry-go-round, a swing, three shooting galleries, a ferris wheel, and an indefinite number of other booths set up, within exactly one foot of the line that divided the public square from the church square.

The owners of the "amusement park" showed him their permits, duly signed by the Mayor, and Don Camillo retired without comment to the rectory. That evening all hell broke loose in the form of barrel organs, loudspeakers, gunfire, shouting and singing, bells, whistling, screaming and bellowing.

Don Camillo went to protest to Christ. "This shows a lack of respect for the house of God."

"Is there anything that is immoral or scandalous?" asked Christ.

"No—merry-go-rounds, swings, little motor cars—chiefly children's amusements."

"Well then, it is simply democracy."

"But this infernal din?" protested Don Camillo.

"The din is democracy too, provided it remains within the law. Outside Church territory, the Mayor is in command, my son."

One side of the rectory adjoined the square, and exactly underneath one of its windows a strange apparatus had been erected. This immediately aroused Don Camillo's curiosity. It was a small column about three feet high, topped by a kind of stuffed mushroom covered with leather. Behind it was another column, taller and more slender, which had a large dial with numbers from 1 to 1000. A blow was struck at the mushroom, and the dial recorded its force. Don Camillo, squinting through the cracks of the shutters, began to enjoy himself.

By eleven o'clock in the evening, the highest number recorded was 750 and that stood to the credit of Badile, the Grettis' cowman, who had fists like sacks of potatoes. Then suddenly Comrade Peppone made his appearance, surrounded by his satellites. All the people came running to watch, crying, "Go on, Peppone, whack it!" Peppone removed his jacket, rolled up his sleeves and took his stand opposite the machine, measuring the distance with his clenched fist.

There was total silence, and even Don Camillo felt his heart hammering.

Peppone's fist sailed through the air and struck the mushroom.

"Nine hundred and fifty," yelled the owner of the machine. "I've seen only one other man get that score and he was a longshoreman in Genoa!" The crowd howled enthusiastically.

Peppone put on his coat again, raised his head and looked up at the shuttered window where Don Camillo was hiding. "To whom it may concern," he remarked loudly, "I might say that a blow that registers nine hundred and fifty is no joke!"

Everyone looked up at the rectory window and laughed. Don Camillo went to bed with his legs shaking under him. The next evening he was there again, peeking from behind his window and waiting feverishly for the clock to strike eleven. Once again, Peppone arrived with his staff, took off his coat, rolled up his sleeves and aimed a mighty blow at the mushroom.

"Nine hundred and fifty-one!" howled the crowd. And once again they looked up at Don Camillo's window and snickered. Peppone also looked up.

"To whom it may concern," he remarked loudly, "I might say that a blow that registers nine hundred and fifty-one is no joke!"

Don Camillo went to bed that night with a temperature.

Next day, he went and knelt before Christ. "Lord," he sighed, "I am being dragged over the precipice!"

"Be strong and resist, Don Camillo!"

That evening, Don Camillo went to his peephole in the window as though he were on his way to the scaffold. The story of Peppone's feat had spread like wildfire, and the whole countryside had come to see the performance. When Peppone appeared there was an audible whisper of "Here he is!" Peppone looked up, jeering, took off his coat, raised his fist and there was silence.

"Nine hundred and fifty-two!"

Don Camillo, when he saw a million eyes fixed on his window, lost the light of reason and hurled himself out of the room.

"To whom . . ." Peppone did not have time to finish; Don Camillo already stood before him. The crowd bellowed and then was suddenly silent.

Don Camillo threw out his chest, took a firm stance, threw away his hat and crossed himself. Then he raised his formidable fist and struck hard.

"One thousand!" yelled the crowd.

"To whom it may concern, I might say that a blow that registers one thousand is no joke," remarked Don Camillo.

Peppone had grown rather pale, and his satellites were glancing at him doubtfully, hesitating between resentment and disappointment. Other bystanders were chuckling delightedly. Peppone looked Don Camillo straight in the eye and took off his coat again. He stepped in front of the machine and raised his fist.

"Lord!" whispered Don Camillo hastily.

Peppone's fist sailed through the air.

"One thousand," bawled the crowd and Peppone's bodyguard rejoiced.

"At one thousand all blows are formidable," observed Smilzo. "I think we'll leave it at that."

Peppone went triumphantly in one direction while Don Camillo walked off triumphantly in the other.

"Lord," said Don Camillo when he knelt before the crucifix. "I thank You. I was scared to death."

"That you wouldn't make a thousand?"

"No, that that pig-headed fool wouldn't make it too. I would have had it on my conscience."

"I knew it, and it was lucky that I came to your help," replied Christ, smiling. "Moreover, Peppone, as soon as he saw you, nearly died for fear you wouldn't reach nine hundred and fifty-two."

"Possibly!" muttered Don Camillo, who now and then liked to appear skeptical.

CRIME AND PUNISHMENT

One morning, as he was leaving the house, Don Camillo discovered that someone had defaced the white wall of the rectory by writing in red letters two feet high *Don Camalo,* which means stevedore and which undoubtedly referred to a feat of strength and daring which Don Camillo had performed a few days before.

It was on Easter morning that Don Camillo had found a colossal chocolate egg tied up with a red silk ribbon on his doorstep. On closer inspection, it turned out to be a formidable egg that resembled chocolate but was actually a two-hundred-pound bomb shorn of its pins and painted a nice rich brown. The donor was not hard to guess, for there was a card attached which read "Happy Eester" and its receipt had been carefully planned. The church square thronged with people all eyeing Don Camillo and enjoying his discomfort.

Don Camillo kicked the egg which, naturally, remained immovable.

"It's pretty heavy!" someone shouted.

"Needs a bomb-removal squad!" suggested another voice.

"Try blessing it and see if it doesn't walk off of its own accord!" cried a third voice.

Don Camillo turned pale and his knees began to tremble. Then he bent down and with his immense hands grasped the bomb by its extremities.

"Lord!" whispered Don Camillo desperately.

"Heave ho! Don Camillo," replied a quiet voice that came from the high altar.

Slowly and implacably Don Camillo straightened his back with the enormous mass of iron in his hands. He stood for a moment contemplating the crowd and then set out. He left the church square and step by step, slow and inexorable as fate, crossed the big square. The crowd followed in silence, amazed. On reaching the far end of the square, opposite the Party headquarters, he stopped. And the crowd stopped, too.

"Lord," whispered Don Camillo desperately.

"Heave ho! Don Camillo," came a rather anxious voice from the now distant high altar of the church.

Don Camillo collected himself, then with one sudden movement brought the great weight up to his chest. Another effort and the bomb began slowly to rise higher, watched by the now frightened crowd.

One moment the bomb was poised above Don Camillo's head, the next it lay on the ground exactly in front of the Party headquarters.

Don Camillo looked at the crowd: "Returned to sender," he observed in a loud voice. "Easter is spelled with an *A*. Correct and redeliver."

The crowd made way for him, and Don Camillo returned triumphantly to the rectory.

Don Camillo savored the memory of this feat, and to find it treated as a public joke in the form of a pun plastered in red letters on the rectory wall hurt a most tender spot, his vanity. He tried to cover the inscription with a bucket of whitewash and a large brush, but it was written in aniline red, so that whitewash was completely useless and the letters only glared more violently. Don Camillo had to resort to scraping, and the job took him easily half the day.

When he went to talk things over he was as white as a baker all over, but in a distinctly black frame of mind. "If I can only find out who did it," he said, "I'll beat the daylights out of him."

"Don't be melodramatic, Don Camillo," Christ advised him. "This is some urchin's doing. After all, no one has really insulted you."

"Do You think it proper to call a priest a stevedore?" protested Don Camillo. "And then, it's the kind of nickname that, if people catch on to it, could stick to me all my life."

"You've got broad shoulders, Don Camillo," Christ consoled him with a smile. "I never had shoulders like yours and yet I bore the cross without beating anybody."

Don Camillo agreed that Christ was right. But he was not satisfied and that evening, instead of going to bed, he stood in a strategic position and waited patiently. Toward two o'clock in the morning an individual appeared in the church square and, with a small pail on the ground beside him, set to work carefully upon the wall of the rectory. Don Camillo didn't give him time even to complete the letter *D* before he overturned the pail on the fellow's head and sent him flying with a terrific kick in the pants.

Aniline dye is an accursed thing, and Smilzo stayed home for three days scrubbing his face with every conceivable concoction. When he did go out and work, he was greeted with the nickname of "Redskin." Don Camillo fanned the flames until he discovered, when it was too late, that the handle of his front door had received a coating of red color. Without saying a word, Don Camillo went and found Smilzo at the tavern and with a blow that was enough to blind an elephant plastered his face with the paint collected from the door handle. Naturally, the affair immediately took on a political aspect, and since Smilzo was supported by half a dozen of his own party, Don Camillo was forced to use a bench in self-defense.

The six who had been routed by Don Camillo's bench were seething, the tavern was in an uproar and that same evening, an unknown person serenaded Don Camillo by throwing a firecracker in front of the rectory door.

Now the transition from firecrackers to grenades is easily made and things did seem to be getting out of hand when, one fine morning, Don Camillo received an urgent summons to the city because the Bishop wished to speak to him.

The Bishop was old and bent and in order to look Don Camillo in the face he had to raise his head considerably. "Don Camillo," he said, "you are not well. You need to spend a few months in a beautiful mountain village. Yes, yes; the parish priest at Puntarossa died recently, and so we can kill two birds with one stone: you will be able to reorganize the parish for me and at the same time you will regain your health. Then you will come back as fresh as a rose. Don Pietro, a young man who will make no trouble, will substitute for you. Are you pleased, Don Camillo?"

"No, Excellency; but I shall leave as soon as Your Excellency wishes."

"Good," replied the Bishop. "Your discipline is the more commendable as you accept without discussion my instructions to do something that is against your personal inclinations."

"Excellency, wouldn't you be displeased if the people of my parish said that I ran away because I was afraid?"

"No," replied the old man, smiling. "Nobody on this earth could ever think that Don Camillo was afraid. Go with God, Don Camillo, and leave benches alone; they never constitute a Christian argument."

The news spread quickly in the village after Peppone announced it in person at a special meeting. "Don Camillo is going," he proclaimed. "Transferred to some Godforsaken mountain village. He is leaving tomorrow afternoon at three o'clock."

"Hurrah!" shouted the entire meeting. "And may he croak when he gets there . . ."

"All things considered, it's the best way out," said Peppone. "He was beginning to think he was the King and the Pope rolled into one. If he had stayed here we would have had to put him in his place. This saves us the trouble."

"And we will let him slink away like a whipped cur," howled

Brusco. "Make the village understand that anyone who is caught on the church square at three o'clock will hear from the Party."

The time came for Don Camillo to say good-by to Christ above the altar. "I wish I could take You with me," sighed Don Camillo.

"I will go with you just the same," replied Christ. "Don't worry."

"Have I really done anything bad enough to deserve being sent away?" asked Don Camillo.

"Yes."

"Then everyone is against me," sighed Don Camillo.

"Everyone," replied Christ. "Even Don Camillo himself disapproves of what you have done."

"That is true enough," Don Camillo acknowledged. "I could hit myself."

"Keep your hands quiet, Don Camillo, and a pleasant journey to you."

In a city, fear can affect fifty per cent of the people, but in a village the percentage is doubled. The roads were deserted. Don Camillo climbed into the train and as he watched his church tower disappear behind a clump of trees he felt very low indeed. "Not even a dog remembered me," he sighed. "It is clear that I have failed in my duties and it is also clear that I am a bad egg."

The train was a local that stopped at every station and therefore it stopped at Boschetto which consisted of five houses about four miles away from Don Camillo's own village. Suddenly, Don Camillo found his compartment invaded, he was hustled to the window and saw a crowd of people clapping their hands and throwing flowers.

"Peppone's men had said that if anyone in the village showed up to see you off it meant trouble," the farmer from Stradalunga explained. "And so to avoid trouble we all came on here to say good-by."

Don Camillo was completely dazed and felt a humming in his ears; when the train moved off the entire compartment was filled with flowers, bottles, bundles and parcels of all sizes, while poultry with their legs tied together clucked and protested from the baggage racks overhead.

But there was still a thorn in his heart. "And the others? They must really hate me to have done such a thing. It wasn't even enough for them to get me sent away!"

Fifteen minutes later the train stopped at Boscoplanche. There Don Camillo heard his name called and going to the window he found Mayor Peppone and his entire gang. Mayor Peppone made the following speech:

"Before you leave it seems to us proper to bring you the greetings of the people and good wishes for a rapid recovery, the which will enable a speedy return to your spiritual mission."

Then, as the train began to move, Peppone took off his hat with a sweeping gesture and Don Camillo also removed his hat and remained standing at the window with it poised in the air like a statue of the Risorgimento.

The church at Puntarossa sat on the top of the mountain and looked like a picture postcard. When Don Camillo reached it, he inhaled the pine-scented air deeply and exclaimed with satisfaction:

"A rest up here will certainly do me good, the which will enable a speedy return to my spiritual mission."

THE RETURN TO THE FOLD

The priest who was sent to substitute in the parish during Don Camillo's political convalescence was young and delicate. He knew his business and he spoke courteously, using lovely polished phrases that seemed to be newly minted. Naturally, even though he knew that he was only in a temporary position, this young priest established some small innovations in the church just as any man will if he is to be tolerably at his ease in strange surroundings.

On the first Sunday following the new priest's arrival, the congregation noticed two important novelties: the great candlestick that held the paschal candle which always stood on the second step at the Gospel side of the altar, had been shifted to the Epistle side and placed in front of a small picture of a saint—a picture which had not been there before.

Out of curiosity and respect for the new priest, the entire village was present, with Peppone and his henchmen in the front pews.

"Look," muttered Brusco to Peppone with a chuckle, pointing out the candlestick, "changes!"

"M-m-m," mumbled Peppone irritably. And he remained irritable until the priest came down to the altar rail to preach.

At that point Peppone had had enough and just as the priest was about to begin, he left his companions, marched up to the candlestick, grasped it firmly, carried it past the altar and placed it in its old position on the second step to the left. Then he returned to his seat in the front row and with knees wide apart and arms folded stared arrogantly straight into the eyes of the young priest.

"Well done!" murmured the entire congregation, not excepting Peppone's political opponents.

The young priest, who had stood open-mouthed watching Peppone's behavior, changed color, stammered somehow through a brief sermon and returned to the altar to complete his Mass.

When he left the church, he found Peppone and his men waiting. The church square was crowded with silent and surly people.

"Listen here, Don . . . Don whatever your name is," said Peppone in an aggressive voice. "Who is this new person whose picture you have hung on the pillar to the right of the altar?"

"Saint Rita of Cascia," stammered the little priest.

"Then let me tell you that this village has no use for Saint Rita of Cascia or of anywhere else. Everything had better be left as it was before."

"I think I am entitled . . ." the young man began, but Peppone cut him short.

"Ah, so that's how you take it? Well, then let me speak clearly: this village has no use for a priest like you."

The young priest gasped. "I cannot see that I have done anything . . ."

"I'll tell you what you've done. You have committed an illegal action. You have attempted to change an order that the permanent priest of the parish established in accordance with the will of the people."

"Hurrah!" shouted the crowd, including the reactionaries.

The little priest attempted a smile. "If that is all that's wrong, everything will be put back exactly as it was before. Isn't that the solution?"

"No!" thundered Peppone, flinging his hat behind him and putting his enormous fists on his hips.

"And may I ask why?"

Peppone had reached the end of his supply of diplomacy. "Well," he said, "if you really want to know, it is not a solution because if I give you a sock on the jaw I would send you flying at least fifteen yards, while if it were the regular incumbent he wouldn't move so much as an inch!"

Peppone didn't go on to explain that if he hit Don Camillo once, the latter would hit him half a dozen times in return. He left it at that but his meaning was clear to all, with the exception of the little priest who merely stared at him in amazement.

"But excuse me," he murmured, "why should you want to hit me?"

Peppone lost patience. "Who in the world wants to hit you? There you go, running down the left-wing parties! I used a figure of speech merely to explain our views. I'm not wasting time hitting a peanut of a priest like you!"

On hearing himself called "a peanut of a priest," the young man drew himself up to his full five feet four inches, his face grew purple and the veins in his neck swelled.

"You may call me a peanut," he cried in a shrill voice, "but I was sent here by ecclesiastical authority and here I shall remain until ecclesiastical authority sees fit to remove me. In this church you have no authority at all! Saint Rita will stay where she is and as for the candlestick, watch what I am going to do!"

He went into the church, grasped the candlestick firmly and after a considerable struggle succeeded in moving it to the Epistle side of the altar in front of the new picture.

"There!" he said triumphantly.

"Very well!" replied Peppone from the church door. Then he turned to the crowd in the church square and shouted: "The people will have something to say about this! To the Town Hall, all of you, and we will make a demonstration of protest."

"Hurrah!" howled the crowd.

Peppone elbowed his way to the front so that he could lead the people, and they followed him yelling and brandishing sticks. When they reached the Town Hall, the yells increased in volume and Peppone yelled also, raising his fist and shaking it at the balcony of the Council Chamber.

"Peppone," shouted Brusco in his ear, "are you crazy? Stop yelling! Have you forgotten that you yourself are the Mayor?"

"Hell . . ." exclaimed Peppone. "When these accursed swine make me lose my head, I don't remember anything!" He ran upstairs and out onto the balcony where he was cheered by the crowd, including the reactionaries.

"Comrades, citizens," shouted Peppone. "We will not suffer this oppression that offends our dignity as free men! We shall remain within the bounds of the law so long as may be possible, but we are going to get justice even if we must resort to gun-fire! In the meantime I propose that a committee of my selection accompany me to the ecclesiastical authorities and impose in a democratic manner the desires of the people!"

"Hurrah!" yelled the crowd, completely indifferent to logic or syntax. "Long live our Mayor Peppone!"

When Peppone and his committee stood before the Bishop, the Mayor had some trouble finding his voice, but at last he got going. "Excellency," he said, "that priest you have sent us is not worthy of the traditions of the leading parish of the district."

The little bent-over Bishop raised his head in order to see the top of Peppone. "Tell me now: what has he been doing?"

Peppone waved his arms. "For the love of God! Doing? He hasn't done anything serious . . . In fact, he hasn't done anything at all . . . The trouble is that . . . Oh well, he's only half a man . . . you know what I mean, a priestling; when that guy is all dressed up, your Eminence must excuse me, but he looks like a coat-hanger loaded with three overcoats and a cloak!"

The old Bishop nodded his head gravely.

"But do you," he asked very graciously, "find out the merits of priests with a tape measure and a weighing machine?"

"No, Excellency," replied Peppone. "We aren't savages! But all the same, how shall I put it—even the eye needs some satisfaction, and in matters of religion it's the same as with a doctor, there's a lot to be said for personal appearance and moral impressions!"

The old Bishop sighed. "Yes, yes, I understand perfectly. But all the same, my dear children, you had a parish priest who looked like a tower and you yourselves came and asked me to remove him!"

Peppone wrinkled his forehead. "Excellency," he explained solemnly, "it was a question of a *casus belli,* an affair *sui generis* as they say. That man was a multiple offense in the way he exasperated us by his provocative and dictatorial poses."

"I know, I know," said the Bishop. "You told me all about it when you were here before, my son, and as you see, I removed him because I fully understood that I had to deal with an unworthy man . . ."

"One moment, if you will excuse me," Smilzo interrupted. "We never said he was an unworthy man! . . ."

"Well, well; if not an unworthy man," continued the Bishop, "at any rate an unworthy priest inasmuch as . . ."

"I beg your pardon," Peppone interrupted, "we never suggested that as a priest he failed in his duty. We only spoke of his serious defects, of his very serious faults as a man."

"Exactly," agreed the old Bishop. "And since the man and the priest are inseparable, and a man such as Don Camillo represents a danger to his neighbors, we are at this very moment considering making his present appointment a permanent one. We will leave him where he is, among the goats at Puntarossa. Yes, we will leave him there, since it has not yet been decided whether he is to be allowed to continue in his functions or whether we shall suspend him *a divinis.* We will wait and see."

Peppone turned to his committee and there was a moment's consultation, then he turned again to the Bishop.

"Excellency," he said in a low voice, and he was sweating and looked pale, as though he found difficulty in speaking audibly. "If the ecclesiastical authority has its own reasons for doing such a thing, of course that is its own affair. Nevertheless, it is my duty to warn your Excellency that until our regular parish priest returns to us, not a soul will enter the church."

The Bishop raised his hands. "But, my sons," he exclaimed, "do you realize the gravity of what you are saying? This is coercion!"

"No, Excellency," Peppone explained, "our decision is simply a question of availing ourselves of democratic liberty. Because we are the only persons qualified to judge whether a priest suits us or not, since we have had to put up with him for nearly twenty years."

"Vox populi vox Dei," sighed the old Bishop. "God's will be done. You can have him back. But don't come whining to me later on about his arrogance."

Peppone laughed. "Excellency! Big bruisers like Don Camillo don't really break any bones. We came here before as a political and social precaution, to make sure that Redskin here didn't lose his head and throw a bomb at him."

"Redskin yourself!" retorted the indignant Smilzo whose face Don Camillo had dyed red and whose head had come in contact with Don Camillo's bench. "I never meant to throw any bombs. I simply threw a firecracker in front of his house to let him know that I couldn't be knocked on the head even by the reverend parish priest in person."

"Ah. Then it was you, my son, who threw the firecracker," said the Bishop mildly.

"Well, Excellency," mumbled Smilzo, "you know how it is. When you've been hit on the head with a bench, you may go too far to get even."

"I understand perfectly," replied the Bishop, who was old and knew how to take people in the right way.

Don Camillo returned ten days later.

"How are you?" asked Peppone, meeting him just as he was leaving the station. "Did you have a pleasant holiday?"

"Well, it was a bit dreary up there. Luckily I took a deck of cards with me and worked off my restlessness playing solitaire," replied Don Camillo. He pulled the cards from his pocket.

"But now I don't need them any more," he said. And delicately, with a smile, he tore the deck in two as though it were a slice of bread.

"We are getting old, Mr. Mayor," sighed Don Camillo.

"To hell with you and those who sent you back here!" muttered Peppone, turning away.

Don Camillo had a lot to tell Christ. Then at the end of their chat, he asked with an air of indifference: "What kind of a fellow was my substitute?"

"A nice lad, cultured and with a sweet nature. When someone did him a good turn, he didn't bait him by tearing up a pack of cards under his nose."

"Lord!" exclaimed Don Camillo, raising his hands. "There are people who have to be thanked that way. I'll bet You that Peppone is saying to his gang right now: 'And he tore the whole pack across, zip, the misbegotten son of an ape!' And he is enjoying saying it! Do You want to bet?"

"No," replied Christ with a sigh, "because that is exactly what Peppone is saying at this moment."

THE DEFEAT

The fight with no holds barred that had been going on for nearly a year was won by Don Camillo, who managed to complete his Recreation Center while Peppone's People's Palace still lacked all its locks.

The Recreation Center was a very up-to-date affair: a hall for social gatherings, dramatic performances, lectures and such activities, a library with a reading and writing room, and a covered area for physical training and winter games. There was a magnificent gymnasium, a track, a swimming pool, and a children's playground with swings. Most of the equipment was as yet in an embryonic stage, but the important thing was to have made a start.

Don Camillo had prepared a lively program for the inauguration ceremony: choral singing, athletic competitions and a game of soccer. For the latter Don Camillo had mustered a really formidable team, a task to which he had brought so much enthusiasm that in the team's eight months of practice the kicks he alone had administered to the eleven players were far more numerous than those all the players put together had succeeded in giving to the ball.

Peppone knew all this and was very angry. He couldn't bear the thought that the party of the people would have to play second fiddle in the celebration organized by Don Camillo on the people's behalf. And when Don Camillo informed him that to show his "sympathetic understanding of the more ignorant social strata of the village" he proposed a match between their "Dynamos" and his own "Knights," Peppone turned pale. He summoned the eleven lads of the local team and made them stand at attention against the wall.

"You are to play against the priest's team. You've got to win or I'll smash in every one of your faces. The Party orders it for the sake of the downtrodden!"

"We'll win!" replied the eleven, sweating with terror.

As soon as he heard this, Don Camillo mustered the "Knights" and addressed them as follows: "We are not uncouth savages like our opponents," he said, smiling pleasantly. "We are capable of reasoning like gentlemen. With the help of God we shall beat them six to nothing. I make no threats; I merely remind you that the honor of the parish is in your hands—and in your feet. If there is some Barabbas among you who is not ready to give his all even to the last drop of his blood, I shall not indulge in Peppone's smashing of faces. I'll simply kick his backside to a pulp!"

The entire countryside attended the inauguration led by Peppone and his satellites with blazing red handkerchiefs round their necks. In his capacity as *Mayor,* he expressed his satisfaction at the event and as *personal representative of the people,* he emphasized his confident belief that the occasion they were celebrating would not be made to serve "unworthy ends of political propaganda such as were already being whispered by evil-minded persons."

During the performance of the choral singers, Peppone was able to point out to Brusco that singing was also a sport, inasmuch as it developed the lungs, and Brusco replied that in his opinion, the exercise would prove even more efficacious as a means of physical development for Catholic youth if they were taught to accompany it with gestures for the improvement not only of their lung power but also of the muscles of their arms.

During the game of basketball, Peppone expressed a sincere conviction that ping-pong too had not only an athletic value, but was so graceful that he was astonished not to find it included in the program.

Since these comments were made in voices that could easily be heard half a mile away, the veins in Don Camillo's neck were very soon swelled to the size of cables. He therefore awaited with indescribable impatience the hour of the soccer match.

At last it was time. White jerseys with a large "K" on the breast for the eleven "Knights." Red jerseys bearing the hammer, sickle and star combined with an elegant "D" adorned the eleven "Dynamos."

The crowd ignored symbols, and hailed the teams in its own way: "Hurrah for Peppone!" or "Hurrah for Don Camillo!" Peppone and Don Camillo looked at one another and exchanged slight and dignified bows.

The referee was a neutral: the clockmaker Binella, apparently a man without political opinions. After ten minutes' play the police sergeant, pale to the gills and followed by his two equally pallid subordinates, approached Peppone.

"Mr. Mayor," he stammered, "don't you think I should telephone to the city for reinforcements?"

"You can telephone for a division for all I care, but if those butchers don't let up, there will be a heap of corpses as high as the first-floor windows! His Majesty the King himself couldn't do a thing about it, do you understand?" howled Peppone, forgetting the very existence of the Republic in his blind fury.

The sergeant turned to Don Camillo who was standing a few feet away. "Don't you think . . ." he stuttered, but Don Camillo cut him short.

"I simply think that nothing short of the personal intervention of the United States of America will prevent us from swimming in blood if those bolsheviks don't stop disabling my men by kicking them in the shins!" he shouted.

"I see," said the sergeant and went off to lock himself in the barracks, although perfectly aware that the usual sequel to such behavior is a general attempt to set fire to the police barracks.

The first goal was made by the Knights, and the crowd sent up a howl that shook the church tower. Peppone, his face distorted with rage, turned on Don Camillo with clenched fists. Don Camillo's fists were already in position. The two of them were within a hair's breadth of conflict, but Don Camillo saw out of the corner of his eye that all other eyes present were fixed upon them.

"If we start fighting, there'll be a free-for-all," he muttered through clenched teeth to Peppone.

"All right, for the sake of the people."

"For the sake of the Faith," said Don Camillo.

Nothing happened. When the first quarter ended a few moments later, Peppone called the Dynamos together. "Fascists!" he said in a voice thick with contempt. Then, seizing hold of Smilzo, the center forward: "As for you, you dirty traitor, suppose you remember that when we were in the mountains I saved your worthless skin three times! If in the next five minutes you haven't made a goal, I'll fix that same skin of yours!"

Smilzo, when play was resumed, got the ball and set to work. And work he did, with his head, with his legs and with his knees. He even bit the ball, he spat his lungs out and split his spleen, and in the fourth minute he sent the ball between the posts.

Then he flung himself on the ground and lay motionless. Don Camillo went to the other side of the field lest his self-control fail him. The Knights' goalkeeper was in a very bad temper.

The Dynamos closed up into a defensive phalanx that seemed impregnable. Thirty seconds before the next break, the referee whistled and a foul was called against the Knights. The ball flew into the air. A child of six could not have muffed it at such an angle. Goal!

The match was over. All Peppone's men had to do now was pick up their injured players and carry them back to the locker rooms. The referee who had no political views left.

Don Camillo was bewildered. He ran off to the church and knelt in front of the altar. "Lord," he said, "why did You fail me? I have lost the match."

"And why should I help you more than the others? Your men had twenty-two legs and so had the Dynamos, Don Camillo, and all legs are equal. Moreover, they are not My business. I am interested in souls. Don Camillo, where are your brains?"

"I can find them with an effort," said Don Camillo. "I was not suggesting that You should have taken charge of my men's legs, which in any case were the best of the lot. But I do say that You did not prevent that dishonest referee from calling an unjust foul against my team."

"The priest can make a mistake in saying Mass, Don Camillo; why do you deny that others can make a mistake and yet be in good faith?"

"Errors happen in most circumstances, but not in sport! When the ball is actually there . . . Binella the clockmaker is a scoundrel . . ." Don Camillo was unable to go on because at that moment he heard an imploring voice and a man came running into the church, exhausted and gasping, his face convulsed with terror.

"They want to kill me," he sobbed. "Save me!"

The crowd had reached the church door and was about to pour into the church itself. Don Camillo seized a weighty candlestick, and brandished it menacingly. "Back! In God's name or I strike!" he shouted. "Remember that anyone who enters here is sacred and immune!"

The crowd hesitated.

"Shame on you, you pack of wolves! Get back to your lairs and pray God to forgive you your savagery."

The crowd stood in silence, heads were bowed and there was a general retreat.

"Make the sign of the cross," Don Camillo ordered them severely, and as he stood there brandishing the candlestick in his huge hand, he looked like Samson.

Everyone made the sign of the cross.

Don Camillo stood back and closed the church door, drawing the bolt, but there was no need. The fugitive had sunk into a pew and was still panting. "Thank you, Don Camillo," he murmured.

Don Camillo made no immediate reply. He paced to and fro for a few moments and then pulled up opposite the man. "Binella!" he said furiously. "Binella, here in my presence and that of God you dare not lie! There was no foul! How much did that heretic Peppone give you to call a foul in a tied game?"

"Two thousand five hundred lire."

"M-m-m-m!" roared Don Camillo, thrusting his fist under his victim's nose.

"But then . . ." moaned Binella.

"Get out," bawled Don Camillo, pointing to the door.

Alone again, Don Camillo turned toward Christ. "Didn't I tell You that the swine had sold himself? Haven't I a right to be mad?"

"None at all, Don Camillo," replied Christ. "You started it when you offered Binella two thousand lire to do the same thing. When Peppone bid five hundred lire more, Binella accepted."

Don Camillo raised his hands. "Lord," he said, "but looking at it that way makes me the guilty man!"

"Exactly, Don Camillo. When you, a priest, made the first offer, he assumed it wasn't wrong and then, quite naturally, he took the more profitable bid."

Don Camillo bowed his head. "And do You mean to tell me that if that unhappy wretch gets beaten up by my men, it will be my fault?"

"In a certain sense, yes, because you were the first to lead him into temptation. Nevertheless, your sin would have been greater if Binella, accepting your offer, had agreed to cheat on behalf of your team. Because then the Dynamos would have done the beating up, and you would have been powerless to stop them."

Don Camillo reflected awhile. "In fact," he said, "it works out better that the others won."

"Exactly, Don Camillo."

"Then, Lord," said Don Camillo, "I thank You for having let me lose. And if I say that I accept the defeat as a punishment for my dishonesty, You must believe that I am really penitent. Because, to see a team like mine, who could easily swallow and digest a couple of thousand Dynamos, to see them beaten . . . is enough to break one's heart, and cries for vengeance to God!"

"Don Camillo!" Christ admonished him, smiling.

"You don't understand me," sighed Don Camillo. "Sport is a thing apart. Either one cares or one doesn't. Do I make myself clear?"

"Only too clear. I understand you so well that . . . Come now, when are you going to get your revenge?"

Don Camillo leaped to his feet, his heart swelling with delight. "Six to nothing!'' he shouted. ''Six to nothing that they never even see the ball! Do You see that confessional?''

He flung his hat up in the air, caught it with a neat kick as it dropped and sent it like a thunderbolt into the little window of the confessional.

''Goal!'' said Christ, smiling.

THE AVENGER

Smilzo rode up on his racing bicycle and braked it by letting his rear end slip off the seat backwards and stop the wheel.

Don Camillo was sitting reading the newspaper on the bench in front of the rectory. He looked up. "Does Stalin hand you down his trousers?" he asked placidly.

Smilzo handed him a letter, touched his cap, leaped on his bicycle and was about to disappear around the corner when he slowed down. "No, the Pope does that," he called, then stood on his pedals and was gone in a flash.

Don Camillo had been expecting the letter. It contained an invitation to the inauguration ceremony of the People's Palace, with a program of the festivities enclosed. Speeches, reports, a band and refreshments. Then in the afternoon: *"Great Boxing Match between the Heavyweight Champion of the Local Section, Comrade Bagotti Mirco, and the Heavyweight Champion of the Provincial Federation, Comrade Gorlini Anteo."*

Don Camillo went off to discuss the event. "Lord!" he exclaimed, when he had read the program aloud. "If this isn't vile! If Peppone weren't an utter boor, he would stage the return match between the Knights and the Dynamos instead of this pommeling bout! I'm going to . . ."

"You're entirely wrong," Christ interrupted him. "It's perfectly logical of Peppone to try something different. Even if his champion loses, he is still all right: one comrade fights another; it all remains in the family. But if your team beat his, it would be detrimental to the prestige of his party. Don Camillo, you must admit that Peppone couldn't possibly have staged a return match."

"And yet," exclaimed Don Camillo, "I did stage a match against his team, and what's more, I lost it!"

"But, Don Camillo," Christ put in gently, "you don't represent a party. Your team was not defending the colors of the Church. Or do you perhaps think that that Sunday afternoon defeat was a defeat for the Catholic Faith?"

Don Camillo began laughing. "Lord," he protested, "You've got me wrong if You accuse me of any such idea. I was only saying, as a sportsman, that Peppone is a boor. And so You will forgive me if I laugh when his famous champion gets such a licking that by the third round he won't know his own name."

"Yes, I shall forgive you, Don Camillo. But I find it less easy to forgive your enjoying the spectacle of two men pounding each other with their fists."

Don Camillo raised his arms. "I have never done anything of the kind. Such manifestations of brutality only foster that cult of violence which is already too deeply rooted in the minds of the masses. I agree with You in condemning any sport in which skill is subordinated to brute force."

"Bravo, Don Camillo," said Christ. "If a man feels the need to limber his muscles, he doesn't have to fight with his neighbor. He can put on a pair of well-padded gloves and take it out on a sack of sawdust or a ball suspended somewhere."

"Exactly," agreed Don Camillo, crossing himself quickly and hurrying away. A little later he passed through the church again.

"Will you satisfy My curiosity, Don Camillo?" called Christ. "What is the name of that leather ball which you have attached to the ceiling of your attic?"

"I believe it is called in English a 'punching bag,' " muttered Don Camillo, stopping for a moment.

"And what does that mean?"

"I don't know any English," replied Don Camillo, making a quick escape.

Don Camillo attended the inaugural ceremony of the People's Palace, and Peppone accompanied him personally upon a tour of the entire grounds; it was all thoroughly up-to-date.

"What do you think of it?" asked Peppone, who was burbling with joy.

"Charming!" replied Don Camillo, smiling cordially. "To tell you the truth I never would have thought that a simple builder like Brusco could have done it."

"True enough!" muttered Peppone, who had spent God only knew how much for the best architect in the city.

"Quite a good idea to make the windows horizontal instead of perpendicular," observed Don Camillo. "The ceilings are not very high but it's not too obvious. And this I suppose is the warehouse."

"It's the Assembly Room," Peppone explained.

"Ah! And have you put the armory and the cells for dangerous adversaries in the basement?"

"No," replied Peppone. "We haven't any dangerous adversaries, they are all harmless little people who can remain in circulation. As for an armory, we thought we would use yours if we needed to."

"An admirable idea," agreed Don Camillo politely. "You have been able to see for yourself how well I look after the Tommy gun which you entrusted to my care, Mr. Mayor."

They had pulled up in front of a huge picture representing a man with a heavy walrus mustache, small eyes and a pipe. "Is that one of your dead leaders?" asked Don Camillo respectfully.

"That is someone who is very much among the living and when he comes will end up sitting on the lightning rod of your own church."

"Too high a position for a humble parish priest. The highest position in a small community always belongs to the Mayor, and from now on I put it at your complete disposal."

"Are we to have the honor of your presence among us at the boxing match today, Reverend Sir?" asked Peppone, thinking it best to change the subject.

"Thank you, but you had better give my seat to someone who is better qualified to appreciate the innate beauty and educational significance of the performance. But I'll be available at the rectory in case your champion needs the Last Rites. Just send Smilzo and I can be with you within a couple of minutes."

During the afternoon, Don Camillo chatted for an hour with Christ and then asked to be excused: "I'm a bit sleepy and I think I'll take a nap. And I thank You for making it rain cats and dogs. The crops needed it."

"And moreover, according to your hopes, it will prevent many people from coming to Peppone's celebration," added Christ. "Am I right?"

Don Camillo shook his head.

But the rain, heavy though it was, didn't dampen Peppone's festivities: people flocked from every section of the countryside, and the gymnasium of the People's Palace was as full as an egg. "Champion of the Federation" was a fine title and Bagotti was popular in the region. And then it was also to a certain extent a match between town and country, and that aroused interest.

Peppone surveyed the crowd triumphantly from the front row. He was sure that at the worst Bagotti could only lose on points, which would be almost as good as a victory.

On the stroke of four, after an outburst of applause and yelling, the gong was sounded and the audience began to get tense and excited.The federal champion surpassed Bagotti in style, but Bagotti was quicker and the first round left the audience breathless. Peppone was pouring with sweat and looked as if he had swallowed dynamite.

The second round began well for Bagotti, who took the offensive, but suddenly he went down in a heap and the referee began the count.

"No," bawled Peppone, leaping to his feet. "It was below the belt!"

The federal champion smiled sarcastically at Peppone. He shook his head and touched his chin with his glove.

"No!" bellowed Peppone in exasperation, drowning the uproar of the audience. "You all saw it! First he hit him low, and when the pain made him double up he gave him a left to the jaw! It was a foul!"

The federal champion shrugged his shoulders and snickered, and meanwhile the referee, having counted up to ten, was grasping the fallen champion's hand in order to pull him to his feet. Then the tragedy occurred.

Peppone threw away his hat and in one bound was in the ring and advanced with clenched fists upon the federal champion. "I'll show you," he howled.

"Give it to him, Peppone," yelled the infuriated crowd.

The boxer put up his fists, and Peppone fell upon him like a Panzer and struck hard. But Peppone was too furious, and his adversary dodged him easily and slugged him one right on the point of the jaw. He put all his weight behind it, as Peppone just stood there motionless and wide open; it was like hitting a sack of sawdust.

Peppone slumped to the floor and the audience froze into silence. But just as the champion smiled compassionately at the giant lying prone on the mat, there was a terrific yell from the crowd as a man entered the ring. Without even bothering to remove his drenched raincoat or cap, he seized a pair of gloves lying on a stool in the corner, pulled them on, and standing on guard squarely before the champion aimed a terrific blow at him. The champion dodged it and danced round the man who simply revolved slowly. Then the champion launched a formidable blow. The other barely moved but parried with his left while his right shot forward like a thunderbolt; the champion was unconscious when he hit the center of the ring.

The crowd went crazy.

It was the bellringer who brought the news to the rectory, and Don Camillo had to leave his bed to open the door because the bellringer seemed to be insane, and if he hadn't been allowed to pour out the whole story from A to Z, there seemed every reason to fear that he would blow up. Don Camillo went downstairs to report.

"Well?" Christ asked. "How did it go?"

"A very disgraceful brawl; such a spectacle of disorder and immorality as You can't imagine!"

"Anything like that time when they wanted to lynch your referee?" asked Christ casually.

Don Camillo laughed. "Referee, my foot! In the second round Peppone's champion slumped like a sack of potatoes. Then Peppone himself jumped into the ring and went for the victor. Naturally, although he is as strong as an ox, he's such a hothead that he slugs like a Zulu or a Russian, and the champion gave him one on the jaw that laid him out cold."

"And so this is the second defeat his section has suffered."

"Two for the section and one for the federation," chuckled Don Camillo. "Because that was not the end! No sooner had Peppone gone down than another man jumped into the ring and fell upon the victor. Must have been somebody from one of the neighboring villages, a fellow with a beard and a mustache who put up his fists and struck out at the federal champion."

"And I suppose the champion dodged and struck back and the bearded man went down too and added to the brutal exhibition," Christ remarked.

"No! The man was as impregnable as an iron safe. So the champion began dodging round trying to catch him off guard and finally, zac! he puts in a straight one with his right. Then I feinted with the left and caught him square with the right and left the ring!"

"And what had you to do with it?"

"I don't understand . . ."

"You said: 'I feinted with the left and caught him square with the right.' "

"I can't imagine how I came to say such a thing."

Christ shook His head. "Could it possibly be because you were the man who struck down the champion?"

"It wouldn't seem so," said Don Camillo gravely. "I have neither beard nor mustache."

"But those of course could be acquired so that the crowd wouldn't suspect that the parish priest is interested in the spectacle of two men fighting in public with their fists!"

Don Camillo shrugged. "All things are possible, Lord, and we must also bear in mind that even parish priests are made of flesh and blood."

Christ sighed. "We are not forgetting it, but if parish priests are made of flesh and blood they themselves should never forget that they are also made of brains. Because if the flesh and blood parish priest wishes to disguise himself in order to attend a boxing match, the priest made of brains prevents him from giving an exhibition of violence."

Don Camillo shook his head. "Very true. But You should also bear in mind that parish priests, in addition to flesh and blood and brains, are also made of another thing. And when that other thing sees a Mayor sent flat before all his own people by a swine from the town who has won by hitting below the belt—which is a sin that cries to Heaven for vengeance—that other thing takes the priest of flesh and blood and the priest of brains and sends the lot of them into the ring."

Christ nodded. "You mean to say that I should bear in mind that parish priests are also made of heart?"

"For the love of Heaven," exclaimed Don Camillo. "I never presume to advise You. But I would point out that nobody knows the identity of the man with the beard."

"Nor do I then," replied Christ with a sigh, "but I wonder if you have any idea of the meaning of 'punching bag'?"

"My knowledge of the English language has not improved, Lord," replied Don Camillo.

"Well, then we must be content without knowing even that," said Christ, smiling. "After all, culture in the long run often seems to do more harm than good. Sleep well, champ."

NOCTURNE WITH BELLS

For some time Don Camillo had felt that he was being watched. On turning round suddenly when he was walking along the street or in the fields, he saw no one, but was convinced that if he had looked behind a hedge or in the bushes he would have found a pair of eyes and everything that goes with them. When he left the rectory on a couple of evenings, he not only heard a sound from behind the door but he caught a glimpse of a shadow.

"Never mind," Christ advised him. "Eyes never did anyone any harm."

"But it would be nice to know whether those two eyes are going about alone or accompanied by a third, for instance one of 9 caliber," sighed Don Camillo. "That is a detail not without its own importance."

"Nothing can defeat a good conscience, Don Camillo."

"I know, Lord," sighed Don Camillo once more, "but the trouble is that people don't usually fire at a conscience but between the shoulders."

However, Don Camillo did nothing about the matter and a little time elapsed, and then late one evening when he was sitting alone in the rectory reading, he "felt" the eyes upon him. There were three of them, and raising his head slowly, he saw first of all the black eye of a revolver and then those of Biondo.

"Do I lift my hands?" inquired Don Camillo quietly.

"I don't want to do you any harm," replied Biondo, thrusting the revolver into his jacket pocket. "I was afraid you might be scared when I came in unexpectedly, and might start shouting."

"I see," replied Don Camillo. "And did it never strike you that by simply knocking at the door you could have avoided all this trouble?"

Biondo didn't reply; he went and leaned over the window sill. Then he turned round suddenly and sat down beside Don Camillo's little table. His hair was ruffled, his eyes deeply circled, and his forehead was damp with sweat.

"Don Camillo," he muttered from behind clenched teeth, "that fellow at the house near the dike; it was me that did him in."

Don Camillo lighted a cigar. "The house near the dike?" he said quietly. "Well; that's an old story, it was a political affair and came within the terms of the amnesty. What are you worrying about? You're all right under the law."

Biondo shrugged his shoulders. "To hell with the amnesty," he said furiously. "Every night when I put my light out I can feel him near my bed, and I can't understand what it means."

Don Camillo puffed a cloud of blue smoke into the air. "Nothing at all, Biondo," he replied with a smile. "Listen, go to sleep with the light on."

Biondo sprang to his feet. "You can jeer at that fool Peppone," he shouted, "but you can't do it at me!"

Don Camillo shook his head. "First, Peppone is not a fool, and second, where you are concerned there is nothing that I can do for you."

"If I must buy candles or make an offering to the Church, I'll pay," shouted Biondo, "but you've got to absolve me. And in any case I'm all right legally!"

"I agree, my son," said Don Camillo mildly. "But the trouble is that no one has ever yet made an amnesty for consciences. Therefore, so far as we are concerned we muddle along in the same old way, and in order to obtain absolution it is necessary to be penitent and then to act in a manner that is deserving of forgiveness. It's a long drawn-out affair."

Biondo sneered. "Penitent? I'm only sorry I didn't bag the lot!"

"That is a province in which I am completely incompetent. On the other hand, if your conscience tells you that you acted rightly then you should be content," said Don Camillo, opening a book and laying it in front of Biondo. "Look, we have very clear commandments that do not exclude politics. Fifth: *Thou shalt not kill.* Seventh: *Thou shalt not steal.*"

"What has that got to do with it?" asked Biondo in a mystified voice.

"Nothing," Don Camillo reassured him, "but I had an idea that you told me that you had killed him, under the cloak of politics, in order to steal his money."

"I never said so!" shouted Biondo, pulling out his pistol and pushing it into Don Camillo's face. "I never said so, but it's true! And if it's true and you dare to tell a living soul, I'll blow you to bits!"

"We don't tell such things even to the Eternal Father," Don Camillo reassured him, "and in any case He knows them better than we do."

Biondo appeared to quiet down. He opened his hand and looked at his weapon. "Now look at that!" he exclaimed, laughing. "I hadn't even noticed that the safety catch was on."

He raised the catch with a careful finger.

"Don Camillo," said Biondo in a strange voice, "I am sick of seeing that fellow standing near my bed. There are only two ways out —either you absolve me or I shoot you." The pistol shook slightly in his hand, and Don Camillo turned rather pale and looked him straight in the eyes.

"Lord," said Don Camillo mentally, "this is a mad dog and he will fire. An absolution given in such conditions is valueless. What do I do?"

"If you're scared, give him absolution," replied the voice of Christ.

Don Camillo folded his arms on his breast. "No, Biondo," said Don Camillo.

Biondo set his teeth. "Don Camillo, give me absolution or I fire."

"No."

Biondo pulled the trigger and the trigger moved but there was no explosion.

Then Don Camillo fired, and this time there was no misfiring because Don Camillo's blows always hit the mark.

Then he tore up the steps of the tower and rang the bells furiously for twenty minutes. And all the countryside declared that Don Camillo had gone mad, with the exception of Christ above the altar who shook His head, smiling, and Biondo who, tearing across the fields like a lunatic, had reached the bank of the river and was about to throw himself into its dark waters. Then he heard the bells.

Biondo turned back because he had heard a Voice that he had never known. And that was the real miracle, because a pistol that misfires is an accident, but a priest who begins to ring joy-bells at eleven o'clock at night is quite another matter.

MEN AND BEASTS

La Grande was an enormous farm with a hundred cows, modern dairy, orchards and all the rest. And everything belonged to old Pasotti, who lived alone. One day the army of farm hands who worked on the place went on strike and, led by Peppone, went en masse to the big house and were interviewed by old Pasotti from a window.

"May God smite you," he shouted, thrusting out his head. "Can't a decent man have peace in this filthy country?"

"A decent man, yes," replied Peppone, "but not profiteers who deny their workmen what is their just due."

"I only admit of dues as fixed by the law," retorted Pasotti, "and I am perfectly within the law."

Then Peppone told him that so long as he refused to grant the concessions demanded, the workers of La Grande would not work. "So you can feed your hundred cows yourself!" Peppone concluded.

"Very well," replied Pasotti. He closed the window and resumed his interrupted slumbers.

This was the beginning of the strike at La Grande, and it was a strike organized by Peppone in person with a squad of overseers, regular watches, pickets and barricades. The doors and windows of the cowhouse were nailed up and seals placed upon them.

On the first day, the cows lowed because they had not been milked. On the second day, they lowed because they had not been milked and because they were hungry, and on the third day, thirst was added to all the rest and the lowing could be heard for miles around. Then Pasotti's old servant came out the back door of the big house and explained to the men on picket duty that she was going to the village to the pharmacy to buy disinfectants. "I have told the master that he can't possibly want to get cholera from the stench when all the cows have died of starvation."

This remark caused quite a lot of head-shaking among the older laborers who had been working for more than fifty years for Pasotti and who knew that he was incredibly pigheaded. And then Peppone himself stepped in to say, with the support of his staff, that if anyone dared go near the cowhouse he would be treated as a traitor to his country.

Toward the evening of the fourth day, Giacomo, the old cowman from La Grande, came to the rectory. "There is a cow due to calve and she is crying out fit to break your heart, and she will certainly die unless someone goes to help her. But if anyone attempts to go near the cowhouse they will break every bone in his body."

Don Camillo went and clung to the altar rails. "Lord," he said, "You must hold onto me or I shall make the march to Rome!"

"Steady! Don Camillo," replied Christ gently. "Nothing is ever gained by violence. You must try to calm these people so that they will listen to reason and avoid acts of violence."

"Very true," sighed Don Camillo. "One must make them listen to reason. All the same, it seems a pity that while one is preaching reason, the cows should die."

Christ smiled. "By violence, you may save a hundred beasts and kill one man. By using persuasion, you may lose the beasts but avoid the loss of that man. Which seems preferable: violence or persuasion?"

Don Camillo who, full of indignation, was reluctant to renounce his idea of a march on Rome, shook his head. "Lord, You are confusing the issue: this is not only a question of the loss of a hundred cows but of the public patrimony, and the death of those animals is a loss for every one of us, good and bad. And it could intensify existing differences and create a conflict in which not only one but twenty men might die."

Christ was not of his opinion. "But if, by reasoning, you avoid one man being killed today, couldn't you also, by reasoning, avoid others being killed tomorrow? Don Camillo, have you lost your faith?"

Don Camillo went out for a walk across the fields because he was restless. And so it happened that quite by chance his ears became more and more painfully aware of the lowing of the hundred cows at La Grande. Then he heard the voices of the men on picket duty at the barricades, and at the end of ten minutes he found himself crawling inside and along the great cement irrigation ditch that passed underneath the wire fence and which was fortunately not in use at that moment.

"And now," thought Don Camillo, "I just need to find someone waiting at the end of this ditch to knock me on the head." But there wasn't anyone there and Don Camillo was left in peace to make his way cautiously in the direction of the farm.

"Halt!" said a voice presently, and Don Camillo jumped behind a tree trunk.

"Halt or I fire!" repeated the voice, which came from behind another tree trunk on the further side of the ditch.

It was an evening of coincidences and Don Camillo, quite by chance, had come prepared.

"Be careful, Peppone, because I'll fire."

"Ah!" muttered the other. "I might have known that you would be mixed up in this business."

"Truce of God," said Don Camillo, "and if either of us breaks it he is damned. I'll count, and when I say 'three' we both jump into that ditch."

"You wouldn't be a priest if you weren't so mistrustful," replied Peppone, and at the count of three he jumped and they found themselves sitting together at the bottom of the ditch.

From the cowhouse came the desperate lowing of the cows, and it was enough to make one cry. "I suppose you enjoy such music," muttered Don Camillo. "A pity that it will stop when all the cows have died. Why not persuade the farm hands to burn the crops and the barns? Just think of poor Pasotti if he were driven to take refuge in some Swiss hotel to spend those millions he has deposited there."

"He'd have to reach Switzerland first!" growled Peppone threateningly.

"Exactly!" exclaimed Don Camillo. "It's about time we did away with that fifth commandment which forbids us to kill! And when one eventually comes face to face with Almighty God one will only have to speak out bluntly: 'That's quite enough from You, my dear Eternal Father, or Peppone will proclaim a general strike and make everyone fold their arms!' By the way, Peppone, how are you going to get the angels to fold their arms? Have you thought of that?"

Peppone's roar vied with that of the expecting cow whose complaints were heart-rending. "You are no priest!" he vociferated. "You are the chief of the Gestapo!"

"The Gestapo is your affair," Don Camillo corrected him.

"You go around by night, in other people's houses, clutching a Tommy gun like a bandit!"

"And what about you?"

"I am in the service of the people!"

"And I in God's service!"

Peppone kicked a stone. "No use trying to argue with a priest! Before you have uttered two words they drag in politics!"

"Peppone," began Don Camillo gently, but the other cut him short.

"Now don't you begin jawing about the national patrimony and rubbish of that kind or as sure as there is a God in Heaven I'll shoot you!" he exclaimed.

Don Camillo shook his head. "No use trying to argue with a red. Before you have uttered two words they drag in politics!"

The cow that was about to calve complained loudly.

"Who goes there?" came a sudden voice from someone very close to the ditch. Then Brusco and two others appeared.

"Go and take a walk along the road to the mill," Peppone ordered them.

"All right," replied Brusco, "but who are you talking to?"

"To your damned soul," roared Peppone furiously.

"That cow that is going to calve is bellowing," muttered Brusco.

"Go and tell the priest about it!" bawled Peppone, "and let her rot! I am working for the interests of the people, not of cows!"

"Keep your hair on, chief," stammered Brusco, making off hastily with his companions.

"Very well, Peppone," whispered Don Camillo, "and now we are going to work for the interests of the people."

"What are you going to do?"

Don Camillo set out quietly along the ditch toward the farm, and Peppone told him to halt or he would get what he was asking for between the shoulders.

"Peppone is as stubborn as a mule," said Don Camillo calmly, "but he doesn't shoot at the backs of poor priests who are doing what God has commanded."

Then Peppone swore blasphemously and Don Camillo turned on him in a flash. "If you don't stop behaving like a goat, I'll give you one on the jaw just as I did to your celebrated federal champion . . ."

"You needn't tell me: I knew all along that it was you. But that was different."

Don Camillo walked along quietly, followed by the other, muttering and threatening to shoot. As they approached the cowbarn, another voice called to them to halt.

"Go to hell!" replied Peppone. "I am here myself now, so you can get along to the dairy."

Don Camillo did not even glance at the cowbarn door with its seals. He went straight up the stairs to the hayloft above it and called in a low voice: "Giacomo."

The old cowman who had come to see him earlier and had related the story of the cow, got up out of the hay. Don Camillo had a flashlight and by shifting a bale of hay they found a trap door.

"Go down," said Don Camillo to the old man, who climbed down and disappeared for some time.

"She's had her calf all right," he whispered when he returned. "I've seen a thousand of them through it and I know more than any vet."

"Now go along home," Don Camillo told the old man and the old man went.

Then Don Camillo opened the trap door again and sent a bale of hay through the opening. "What do you think you are doing?" asked Peppone who had so far remained hidden.

"Help me to throw down these bales and I'll tell you."

Grumbling as he did so Peppone set to work chucking down the bales, and when Don Camillo jumped down after them into the cowbarn, Peppone followed him.

Don Camillo carried a bale to the right-hand manger. "You'd better attend to the left-hand mangers," he said to Peppone.

"Not if you murder me!" shouted Peppone, seizing a bale and carrying it to the manger.

They worked like an army. Then there was the problem of watering the animals and, since they were dealing with a modern cowbarn with drinking troughs placed along the outer walls, it involved turning one hundred cows right around and then trying to stop them from drinking themselves to death.

When they finished it was still pitch dark in the cow house but that was merely because all the shutters of the windows had been sealed from the outside.

"It's three o'clock in the afternoon," said Don Camillo, looking at his watch. "We'll have to wait until evening before we can get out!"

Peppone was in a fury, but there was nothing for it but patience. When evening fell, Peppone and Don Camillo were still playing cards by the light of an oil lamp.

"I'm so hungry I should swallow a bishop whole!" exclaimed Peppone savagely.

"Hard on the digestion, Mr. Mayor," replied Don Camillo quietly, though he himself was faint with hunger and could have devoured a cardinal. "Before saying you're hungry you should fast for as many days as these cows."

Before leaving, they again filled the mangers with hay. Peppone tried to resist, saying that it was betraying the people, but Don Camillo was inflexible.

And so it happened that during the night there was a deathly silence in the cowbarn and old Pasotti, hearing no more lowing from the cows, was afraid that they were so far gone that they hadn't even the strength to complain. In the morning, he made a move to settle with Peppone, and with some give and take on both sides the strike was settled.

In the afternoon, Peppone turned up at the rectory.

"Well," said Don Camillo in honeyed tones. "You revolutionaries should always listen to your old parish priest. You really should, my dear children."

Peppone stood with folded arms, speechless. Then he blurted out: "But my Tommy gun, reverendo!"

"Your Tommy gun?" replied Don Camillo with a smile. "I'm afraid I don't understand. You had it yourself."

"Yes, I had it when we were leaving the cowbarn, but then you took advantage of my exhaustion and stole it from me."

"Now that you mention it, I believe you're right," replied Don Camillo with disarming candor. "You must forgive me, Peppone, but the truth is that I am getting old and I don't seem able to remember where I've put it."

"Reverendo!" exclaimed Peppone indignantly. "But that's the second one you've swiped from me!"

"Never mind, my son. Don't worry. You will easily find another. Who knows how many you have even now lying around your house!"

"You are one of those priests that, one way or another, compel a decent man to become a Mohammedan!"

"Very possibly," replied Don Camillo, "but then you, Peppone, are not a decent man." Peppone flung his hat on the ground.

"If you were a decent man," the priest went on, "you would be thanking me for what I have done for you and for the people."

Peppone picked up his hat, jammed it on his head and turned away. "You can rob me of two hundred thousand Tommy guns, but when the time comes I will always have a 75 to train on this infernal house!"

"And I'll always find an 81 mortar with which to retaliate," replied Don Camillo calmly.

As Peppone was passing the open door of the church he could see the altar, and angrily pulled off his hat and then crammed it on again quickly for fear someone should see him.

But Christ saw it, and when Don Camillo came in He said gaily: "Peppone went by just now and took off his hat to Me."

"You be careful, Lord," replied Don Camillo. "Remember someone kissed You and then sold You for thirty pieces of silver. That fellow who took off his hat told me only three minutes before that when the time came he would always find a 75 to fire on the house of God!"

"And what did you reply?"

"That I would always manage to find an 81 mortar to fire on his headquarters."

"I understand, Don Camillo. But the trouble is that you have that mortar already."

Don Camillo spread out his arms. "Lord," he said, "there are so many odds and ends a man hates to throw away because of old memories. All of us are a bit sentimental. And then, in any case, isn't it better that a thing like that be in my house rather than in someone else's?"

"Don Camillo is always right," smiled Christ, "just as long as he plays fair."

"No fear about that; I have the best adviser in the universe," replied Don Camillo, and to this Christ could make no reply.

THE PROCESSION

Once every year, for the blessing of the village, the crucifix from above the altar was carried in procession as far as the river bank, where the river also was blessed so that it would refrain from excesses and behave decently.

This year, as Don Camillo was thinking over the final touches to be given to the celebrations, Smilzo stopped in at the rectory.

"The secretary of our local section," said Smilzo, "sends me to inform you that the entire section will take part in the procession complete with all its banners."

"Convey my thanks to Secretary Peppone," replied Don Camillo.

"I am only too happy to have all the men of the section present. But they must be good enough to leave their banners at home. Political banners have no place in religious processions. Those are the orders that I have received."

Smilzo retired and very soon Peppone arrived, red in the face and with his eyes popping out of his head. "We are just as much Christians as the rest of them!" he shouted, bursting in without even knocking on the door. "In what way are we different from other people?"

"In not taking off your hats when you come into other people's houses," said Don Camillo quietly.

Peppone snatched his hat from his head.

"Now you are just like any other Christian," said Don Camillo.

"Then why can't we join the procession with our flag?" shouted Peppone. "Is it the flag of thieves and murderers?"

"No, Comrade Peppone," Don Camillo explained, lighting his cigar. "But the flag of a party cannot be admitted. This procession is concerned with religion and not with politics."

"Then the flags of Catholic Action should also be excluded!"

"And why? Catholic Action is not a political party, as proved by the fact that I am its local secretary. Indeed I strongly advise you and your comrades to join it."

Peppone jeered. "If you want to save your black soul, you had better join our party!"

Don Camillo raised his hands. "Supposing we leave it at that," he replied, smiling. "We all stay as we are and remain friends."

"You and I have never been friends," Peppone asserted.

"Not even when we were in the mountains together?"

"No! That was merely a strategic alliance. For the triumph of our arms one can make an alliance even with priests."

"Very well," said Don Camillo calmly. "Nevertheless, if you want to join in the procession, you must leave your flag at home."

Peppone ground his teeth. "If you think you can play the dictator, reverendo, you're making a big mistake!" he exclaimed. "Either our flag marches or there won't be any procession!"

Don Camillo was not impressed. "He'll get over it," he said to himself. And in fact, during the three days preceding the Sunday of the blessing nothing more was said about the flag. But on Sunday, an hour before Mass, scared people began to arrive at the rectory. Early that morning, Peppone's gang had called at every house in the village with the warning that anyone who took part in the procession would do so at the risk of life and limb.

"No one has said anything of the kind to me," replied Don Camillo. "I am therefore not interested."

The procession was to take place immediately after Mass, and while Don Camillo was vesting for it in the sacristy he was interrupted by a group of parishioners.

"What are we going to do?" they asked him.

"We are going in procession," replied Don Camillo quietly.

"But those ruffians are quite capable of throwing bombs," they objected. "In our opinion you ought to postpone the procession, give notice to the public authorities of the city and have the procession as soon as there are enough police on the spot to protect the people."

"I see," remarked Don Camillo. "And in the meantime we might explain to the martyrs of our Faith that they made a big mistake in behaving as they did and that instead of going off to spread Christianity when it was forbidden, they should have waited quietly until they had police to protect them."

Then Don Camillo showed his visitors the way to the door and they went off, muttering and grumbling.

Shortly afterward a number of aged men and women entered the church. "We are coming along, Don Camillo," they said.

"You are going straight back to your houses!" replied Don Camillo. "God will take note of your pious intentions, but this is decidedly one of those occasions when old men, old women and children should remain at home."

A number of people lingered in front of the church, but when the sound of firing was heard in the distance (Smilzo had let off a Tommy gun into the air as a demonstration), even the group of survivors melted away. Don Camillo found the square as bare as a billiard table.

"Are we going now, Don Camillo?" asked Christ from above the altar. "The river must be beautiful in this sunshine. I'll enjoy seeing it."

"We're going all right," replied Don Camillo. "But I am afraid that this time I shall be the entire procession. If You can put up with that . . ."

"Where there is Don Camillo he is sufficient in himself," said Christ, smiling.

Don Camillo hastily put on the leather harness with the support for the foot of the cross, lifted the enormous crucifix from the altar and adjusted it in the socket. Then he sighed: "All the same, they need not have made this cross quite so heavy."

"You're telling Me!" replied the Lord, smiling. "And I never had shoulders such as yours."

A few moments later Don Camillo, bearing his enormous crucifix, emerged solemnly from the door of the church. The village was completely deserted; people were cowering in their houses and watching through the cracks of the shutters.

"I must look like one of those friars who used to carry a big black cross through villages smitten by the plague," said Don Camillo to himself. Then he began a psalm in his ringing baritone, which seemed to acquire volume in the silence.

After crossing the square he began to walk down the main street, and here again was emptiness and silence. A small dog came out of a side street and began quietly to follow Don Camillo.

"Go away!" muttered Don Camillo.

"Let it alone," whispered Christ from His cross. "Then Peppone won't be able to say that not even a dog walked in the procession."

The street curved and then came the lane that led to the river bank. Don Camillo had no sooner turned the bend when he found the way unexpectedly obstructed. Two hundred men had collected and stood silently across it with folded arms. In front of them stood Peppone, his hands on his hips.

Don Camillo wished he were a tank. But since he could only be Don Camillo, he advanced until he was within a yard of Peppone and then halted. Then he lifted the enormous crucifix from its socket and raised it in his hands, brandishing it as though it were a club.

"Lord," cried Don Camillo. "Hold on tight; I am going to strike!"

But there was no need, because the men scattered before him and the way lay open. Only Peppone, his arms akimbo and his legs wide apart, remained in the middle of the road. Don Camillo put the crucifix back in its socket and marched straight at him and Peppone moved to one side.

"I'm not shifting myself for your sake, but for His," said Peppone, pointing to the crucifix.

"Then take that hat off your head!" replied Don Camillo without so much as looking at him. Peppone pulled off his hat, and Don Camillo marched solemnly through two rows of Peppone's men.

When he reached the river bank he stopped. "Lord," said Don Camillo in a loud voice, "if the few decent people in this filthy village could build themselves a Noah's Ark and float safely upon the waters, I would ask You to send a flood that would break down this dike and submerge the whole countryside. But as these few decent folk live in brick houses exactly like those of their rotten neighbors, and as it would not be just that the good should suffer for the sins of scoundrels like Mayor Peppone and his gang of Godless brigands, I ask You to save this countryside from the river's waters and to give it every prosperity."

"Amen," came Peppone's voice from just behind him.

"Amen," came the response of all the men who had followed the crucifix.

Don Camillo set out on the return journey and when he reached the doorway of the church and turned around so that Christ might bestow a final blessing upon the distant river, he found standing before him: the small dog, Peppone, Peppone's men and every inhabitant of the village, not excluding the druggist, who was an atheist, but who felt that never in his life had he dreamed of a priest like Don Camillo, who could make even the Eternal Father quite tolerable.

THE MEETING

As soon as Peppone read a notice posted at the street corners announcing that a stranger from the city had been invited by the local section of the Liberal Party to hold a meeting in the square, he leaped into the air.

"Here, in the red stronghold! Are we to tolerate such a provocation?" he bawled. "We'll see who commands here!"

Then he summoned his General Staff and the stupendous announcement was studied and analyzed. The proposal to set fire to the headquarters of the Liberal Party was rejected. That of forbidding the meeting met with the same fate.

"That's democracy for you!" said Peppone sententiously. "When an unknown scoundrel can speak in a public square!"

They decided to remain within the bounds of law and order: general mobilization of all members, organization of squads to supervise things generally and avoid any ambush. Occupation of strategic points and protection of their own headquarters. Pickets were to stand by to summon reinforcements from neighboring sectors.

"The fact that they are holding a public meeting here shows that they are confident of overpowering us," said Peppone. "But they will not find us unprepared."

Scouts placed along the roads leading to the villages were to report any suspicious movement, and were already on duty from early that Saturday morning, but they failed to sight so much as a cat throughout the entire day. During the night Smilzo discovered a questionable character on a bike, but he proved to be only a normal drunk. The meeting was to take place Sunday afternoon, but up until three o'clock not a soul showed up.

"They will be coming on the three fifty-five train," said Peppone. And he placed a large contingent of his men in and around the railroad station. The train steamed in and the only person who got off was a thin little man carrying a small canvas suitcase.

"It's obvious that they got wind of something and didn't feel strong enough to meet the emergency," said Peppone.

At that moment the little man came up to him and taking off his hat politely asked if Peppone would be so kind as to direct him to the headquarters of the Liberal Party.

Peppone stared at him in amazement. "The headquarters of the Liberal Party?"

"Yes," explained the little man, "I am due to make a short speech in twenty minutes' time and I don't want to be late."

Everybody was looking at Peppone and Peppone scratched his head. "It is really rather difficult to explain, because the center of the village is a mile away."

The little man looked very unhappy. "Is it possible to find some means of transportation?"

"I have a truck outside," muttered Peppone, "if you want to come along."

The little man thanked him. Then, when they got outside and he saw the truck full of surly faces, red handkerchiefs and Communist badges, he looked at Peppone.

"I am their leader," said Peppone. "Get up in front with me."

Halfway to the village, Peppone stopped the engine and examined his passenger, who was a middle-aged gentleman, very thin and with clear-cut features. "So you are a Liberal?"

"I am," replied the gentleman.

"And you are not alarmed at finding yourself alone here among fifty Communists?"

"No," replied the man quietly. A threatening murmur came from the men in the lorry.

"What have you got in that suitcase?"

The man began to laugh and opened the case. "Pajamas, a pair of slippers and a toothbrush," he exclaimed.

Peppone pushed his hat onto the back of his head and slapped his thigh. "You must be nuts!" he bellowed. "Why aren't you afraid?"

"Simply because I am alone and there are fifty of you," the little man explained quietly.

"What the hell has that got to do with it?" howled Peppone. "Doesn't it strike you that I could pick you up with one hand and throw you into that ditch?"

"No, it doesn't strike me," replied the little man as quietly as before.

"Then you really must either be weak in the head, or irresponsible, or out to bait us."

The little man laughed again. "It's much simpler than that," he said. "I'm just an ordinary, decent man."

"Ah no, my good sir!" exclaimed Peppone. "If you were an ordinary, decent man, you wouldn't be an enemy of the people! A slave of reaction! An instrument of capitalism!"

"I am nobody's enemy and nobody's slave. I am merely a man who thinks differently from you."

Peppone started the engine and the truck lurched forward. "I suppose you made your will before coming here?" he jeered as he jammed his foot on the accelerator.

"No," replied the little man, unperturbed. "All I have is my work and if I should die, I couldn't leave it to anyone else."

Before entering the village, Peppone pulled up for a moment to speak to Smilzo, who was acting as orderly on his motor-bike. Then, by way of several side streets, they reached the headquarters of the Liberal Party. The doors and windows were closed.

"Nobody here," said Peppone gloomily.

"They must all be in the square, of course. It is already late," retorted the little man.

"I suppose that's it," replied Peppone, winking at Brusco.

When they reached the square, Peppone and his men got out of the truck, surrounded the little man and forced their way through the crowd to the platform. The little man climbed onto it and found himself face to face with two thousand men, all wearing the red handkerchief.

He turned to Peppone, who had followed him on to the platform. "Excuse me," he inquired, "but have I by any chance come to the wrong meeting?"

"No," Peppone reassured him. "The fact is that there are only twenty-three Liberals in the whole district and they don't show up much in a crowd. To tell you the truth, if I had been in your place, it would never have entered my head to hold a meeting here."

"It seems obvious that the Liberals have more confidence in the democratic discipline of the Communists than you have," replied the little one.

Peppone looked disconcerted for a moment, then he went up to the microphone. "Comrades," he shouted. "I wish to introduce to you this gentleman, who will make you a speech that will send you all off to join the Liberal Party."

A roar of laughter greeted this introduction and as soon as it died down the little man began speaking.

"I want to thank your leader for his courtesy," he said, "but it is my duty to explain to you that his statement does not express my wishes. Because if at the end of my speech you all went to join the Liberal Party, I would feel it incumbent upon me to go and join the Communist Party, and that would be against all my principles."

He was unable to continue, because at that moment a tomato whistled through the air and struck him in the face.

The crowd began jeering, and Peppone turned white. "Anyone who laughs is a swine!" he shouted into the microphone, and there was immediate silence.

The little man had not moved and was trying to clean his face with his hand. Peppone was a child of instinct and quite unconsciously was capable of magnificent impulses; he pulled his handkerchief from his pocket, then he put it back again and unknotted the vast red kerchief from his neck and offered it to the little man.

"I wore it in the mountains," he said. "Wipe your face."

"Bravo, Peppone!" thundered a voice from the first-floor window of a neighboring house.

"I don't need the approval of the clergy," replied Peppone arrogantly, while Don Camillo bit his tongue with fury at having let his feelings get the better of him.

Meanwhile, the little man had shaken his head, bowed and approached the microphone. "There is too much history attached to that handkerchief for me to soil it with the traces of a vulgar episode that belongs to the less heroic chronicles of our times," he said. "A handkerchief such as we use for a common cold suffices for such a purpose."

Peppone flushed scarlet and also bowed, and then a wave of emotion swept the crowd and there was vigorous applause while the hooligan who had thrown the tomato was kicked off the square.

The little man resumed his speech calmly. He was quiet, without any trace of bitterness; smoothing off corners, avoiding contention. At the end he was applauded, and when he stepped down from the platform a way was cleared before him.

When he reached the far end of the square and found himself beneath the portico of the Town Hall, he stood helplessly with his suitcase in his hand, not knowing where to go or what to do. At that moment Don Camillo hurried up to Peppone, who was standing just behind the man. "You've lost no time, have you, you Godless rascal, in making up to this Liberal priest-eater."

"What?" gasped Peppone, turning toward the little man. "Then you are a priest-eater?"

"But . . ." stammered the man.

"Hold your tongue," Don Camillo interrupted him. "You ought to be ashamed, you who demand a free church in a free state!"

The little man attempted to protest, but Peppone cut him short before he could utter a word. "Bravo!" he bawled. "Give me your hand! When a man is a priest-eater he is my friend, even if he is a Liberal reactionary!"

"Hurrah!" shouted Peppone's satellites.

"You are my guest!" said Peppone.

"Nothing of the kind," retorted Don Camillo. "This gentleman is my guest. I am not a boor who fires tomatoes at his adversaries!"

Peppone pushed himself menacingly in front of Don Camillo. "I have said that he is my guest," he repeated fiercely.

"And as I have said the same thing," replied Don Camillo, "it means that if you want to come to blows with me about it, I'll give you those due to your ruffian Dynamos!"

Peppone clenched his fists.

"Come away," said Brusco. "In another minute you'll be boxing with the priest in the public square!"

The question was settled in favor of a meeting on neutral territory. All three of them went out into the country to luncheon with Gigiotto, a host completely indifferent to politics, and thus even the democratic encounter led to no results of any kind.

ON THE RIVER BANK

Between one and three o'clock of an August afternoon, the heat in those fields of hemp and buckwheat can be both seen and felt. It is almost as though a great curtain of boiling glass hung a few inches from your nose. If you cross a bridge and look down into the canal, you find its bed dry and cracked, with here and there a dead fish, and when you look at a cemetery from the road along the river bank you almost seem to hear the bones rattling beneath the boiling sun. Along the main road you will meet an occasional wagon piled high with sand, with the driver sound asleep lying face downwards on top of his load, his stomach cool and his spine incandescent, or he will be sitting on the shaft fishing out pieces from half a watermelon that he holds on his knees like a bowl.

Then when you come to the big bank, there lies the great river, deserted, motionless and silent, like a cemetery of dead waters.

Don Camillo was walking in the direction of the big river, with a large white handkerchief inserted between his head and his hat. It was half-past one of an August afternoon, and seeing him thus, alone on the white road, under the burning rays of the sun, it was not possible to imagine anything blacker or more blatantly priestlike.

"If there is anyone within a radius of twenty miles who is not asleep at this moment, I'll eat my hat," said Don Camillo to himself. Then he climbed over the bank and sat down in the shade of a thicket of acacias and watched the water shining through the foliage. Presently he took off his clothes, folding each garment carefully and rolling them all into a bundle which he hid among the bushes. Then, wearing only his underdrawers, he plunged into the water.

Everything was perfectly quiet, no one could have seen him because, in addition to selecting the hour of siesta, he had also chosen the most secluded spot. In any case, he was prudent and, at the end of half an hour, he climbed out of the water among the acacias and reached the bush where he had hidden his clothes—only to discover that the clothes were no longer there.

Don Camillo felt his breath fail him.

There could be no question of theft: nobody could possibly want an old faded cassock. It must mean that some deviltry was afoot. And in fact at that very moment he heard voices approaching from the top of the bank. He made out a crowd of young men and girls and then he recognized Smilzo as their leader and was seized with an almost uncontrollable desire to break a branch from the acacias and use it on their backs. But he realized that he would only be playing into the hands of his adversaries—letting them enjoy the spectacle of Don Camillo in his drawers.

So he dived back into the water and swimming beneath the surface reached a little island in the middle of the river. Creeping ashore, he disappeared among the reeds.

Although his enemies hadn't seen him land they flung themselves down along the bank and lay waiting for him, laughing and singing. Don Camillo was in a state of siege.

Don Camillo sat among the reeds and waited. Peppone, followed by Brusco, Bigio and his entire staff, arrived and Smilzo explained the situation with gestures. There was much laughter. Then more people came, and Don Camillo realized that the Mayor's party were out to make him pay dearly. They had hit upon the best system of all because, when anyone makes himself ridiculous, nobody is ever afraid of him again, not even if his fists weigh a ton and he represents the Eternal Father. Don Camillo felt it was grossly unfair because he had never wanted to frighten anyone except the Devil. But somehow politics had contrived so to distort facts that the Communists had come to consider the parish priest as their enemy and to say that if things were not as they wished it was all the fault of the priests. When things go wrong, it sometimes seems less important to find a remedy than to find a scapegoat.

"Lord!" said Don Camillo. "I am ashamed to address You in my underdrawers, but my position is becoming serious and if it is not a mortal sin for a poor parish priest who is dying of the heat to go bathing, please help me, because I am quite unable to help myself."

The watchers had brought flasks of wine, baskets of food and an accordion; it was obvious that they hadn't the faintest intention of raising the siege. In fact they had extended it so that they spread along the river's bank up to the ford. Here the shore was covered with scrub and underbrush. Not a soul had set foot in this area since 1945 because the retreating Germans had mined both sides of the bank at the ford. The authorities, after several disastrous attempts at removing the mines, finally isolated the area with posts and barbed wire.

Therefore, that section of the shore upstream from Don Camillo was well guarded by a mine-field, and he knew that if he swam downstream beyond Peppone's men he would end up in the middle of the village.

So Don Camillo did not move; he remained lying on the damp earth, chewing a reed and sorting out his thoughts.

"Well," he concluded, "a respectable man remains a respectable man even in his drawers. If he performs some reputable action, then his clothing ceases to have any importance."

The daylight was beginning to fade and the watchers on the bank lit torches and lanterns. As soon as the underbrush was veiled in shadow, Don Camillo slid into the water and made his way cautiously upstream until his feet touched bottom at the ford. Then he struck out for the bank, lifting his mouth out of the water from time to time to catch his breath.

He reached the shore but now the problem was to get out of the water without being seen; once among the bushes he could easily reach the bank and by running along it, duck between rows of vines and through the buckwheat and so reach his own garden.

He grabbed a bush and pulled himself up slowly, but just as he was almost out, the bush came up by the roots and Don Camillo was back in the water. At the splash people came running. But in a flash Don Camillo leaped ashore and vanished among the bushes.

There were loud cries and the entire crowd rushed toward the spot, and the moon rose to shed its light on the spectacle.

"Don Camillo!" shouted Peppone, thrusting his way to the front of the crowd. "Don Camillo!" There was no reply and a deathly silence fell upon all those present.

"Don Camillo!" yelled Peppone again. "For God's sake don't move! You are in the mine-field!"

"I know I am," replied the voice of Don Camillo quietly, from behind a small shrub in the midst of the sinister shrubbery.

Smilzo came forward carrying a bundle. "Don Camillo," he shouted, "it was a rotten trick. Keep still and here are your clothes."

"My clothes? Oh, thank you, Smilzo. If you will be so kind as to bring them to me."

A branch moved at the top of a bush some distance away. Smilzo's mouth fell open and he looked round at those behind him. The silence was broken only by an ironical laugh from Don Camillo.

Peppone seized the bundle from Smilzo's hand. "I'll bring them," said Peppone, advancing slowly toward the posts and the barbed wire. He had one leg over the barrier when Smilzo sprang forward and dragged him back.

"No, chief," said Smilzo, taking the bundle from him and entering the enclosure. "I will."

The people shrank back, their faces were damp with sweat and they held their hands over their mouths. Amid a leaden silence, Smilzo made his way slowly toward the middle of the enclosure, placing his feet carefully.

"Here you are," said Smilzo, in a ghost of a voice, as he reached Don Camillo's bush.

"Good!" muttered Don Camillo. "And now you can come round here. You have earned the right to see me in my drawers." Smilzo obeyed him.

"Well? And what do you think of a parish priest in drawers?"

"I don't know," stammered Smilzo. "I've stolen trifles and I've socked a couple of guys, but I've never really hurt anyone."

"Ego te absolvo," replied Don Camillo, making the sign of the cross on his forehead. They walked slowly toward the bank and the crowd held its breath and waited for the explosion.

They climbed over the barbed wire and walked along the road, Don Camillo leading and Smilzo, at his heels, still walking on tiptoe as if in the mine-field because he no longer knew what he was doing. Suddenly Smilzo collapsed on the ground. Peppone, leading the rest of the people, picked Smilzo up by the collar as he went by and dragged him along like a bundle of rags, without once taking his eyes from Don Camillo's back. At the church door Don Camillo turned round for a moment, bowed politely to his parishioners and went into the church.

The others left in silence and Peppone remained standing alone before the church, staring at the closed door and still clutching the collar of the unconscious Smilzo. Then he shook his head, and turned and went his way, still dragging his burden.

"Lord," whispered Don Camillo, "one must serve the church, even by protecting the dignity of a parish priest in his drawers."

There was no reply.

"Lord," whispered Don Camillo anxiously, "did I really commit a mortal sin by going swimming?"

"No," replied Christ, "but you did commit a mortal sin when you dared Smilzo to bring you your clothes."

"I never thought he would do it. I was thoughtless."

From the direction of the river came the sound of a distant explosion. "Every now and then a rabbit runs through the mine-field, and then . . ." Don Camillo explained in an almost inaudible voice. "So we must conclude that You . . ."

"You must conclude nothing at all, Don Camillo," Christ interrupted him with a smile. "With the temperature you are running at this moment, your conclusions would scarcely be of any value."

Meanwhile, Peppone had reached the door of Smilzo's home. He knocked and the door was opened by an old man who made no comment as Peppone handed over his burden. And it was at that moment that Peppone also heard the explosion, shook his head and remembered many things. Then he took Smilzo back from the old man for a moment and boxed his ears until his hair stood on end.

"Forward! Charge!" murmured Smilzo in a faraway voice as the old man took him again.

RAW MATERIAL

One afternoon Don Camillo, who for the past week had been in a chronic state of agitation and done nothing but rush around, was returning from a visit to a neighboring village. When he reached his own parish, he had to get off his bicycle because some men had appeared since his departure and were digging a ditch right across the road.

"We are putting in a new drain," a workman explained, "by the Mayor's orders."

Don Camillo went straight to the Town Hall and when he found Peppone, he lost his temper. "Are we all going off our nuts?" he exclaimed. "Here you are, digging this filthy ditch. Don't you know that this is Friday?"

"Well!" replied Peppone with astonishment. "And is it forbidden to dig a ditch on a Friday?"

Don Camillo roared: "But don't you realize that it's less than two days to Sunday?"

Peppone looked worried. He rang a bell and Smilzo came in. "Hey, Smilzo," said Peppone. "The reverendo says that since today is Friday, it's less than two days to Sunday. What do you think?"

Smilzo pondered seriously. Then he pulled out a pencil and made calculations on a piece of paper. "Why," he said presently, "taking into consideration that it is now four o'clock in the afternoon and therefore within eight hours of midnight, it will actually be Sunday within thirty-two hours from the present time."

Don Camillo watched all these maneuvers and by now was almost frothing at the mouth. "I understand!" he shouted. "This is a put-up job to boycott the Bishop's visit."

"Reverendo," replied Peppone, "where is the connection between our local sewage and the Bishop's visit? And also, may I ask what bishop and why he should be coming here?"

"To the devil with your black soul!" bawled Don Camillo. "That ditch must be filled in at once, or else the Bishop will be unable to pass on Sunday!"

Peppone's face looked completely blank. "Unable to pass? But then how did you pass? There are a couple of planks across the ditch, if I am not mistaken."

"But the Bishop is coming by car," exclaimed Don Camillo. "We can't ask a bishop to get out of his car and walk!"

"You must forgive me, I didn't know that bishops were unable to walk," retorted Peppone. "If that is so then it is quite another matter. Smilzo, call the city and tell them to send us a crane immediately. We'll put it near the ditch and as soon as the Bishop's car arrives the crane can grapple onto it and lift it over the ditch. Understand?"

"Perfectly, chief. And what color crane should I ask for?"

"Tell them chromium or nickel-plated; it will look better."

In such circumstances even a man who lacked Don Camillo's armor-plated fists might have been tempted to come to blows. But it was precisely in such cases as these that Don Camillo, on the contrary, became entirely composed. His argument to himself was as follows: "If this fellow sets out so deliberately to provoke me, it is because he hopes that I will lose my temper. Therefore, if I give him one on the jaw I am simply playing his game. As a fact, I should not be striking Peppone, but a Mayor in the exercise of his functions, and that would make an infernal scandal and create an atmosphere not only hostile to me personally but also to the Bishop."

"Never mind," he said quietly, "even bishops can walk."

Speaking in church that evening, he implored his congregation to remain calm, to concentrate on asking God to shed light upon the mind of their Mayor so that he would not ruin the impending ceremony by compelling the faithful to pass one at a time over a couple of insecure boards. And they must also pray God to prevent this improvised bridge from breaking under the undue strain and thus turning a day of rejoicing into one of mourning.

This Machiavellian sermon had its calculated effect upon all the women of the congregation who, on leaving the church, collected in front of Peppone's house and carried on to such an extent that at last Peppone came to a window and shouted that they could all go to hell and that the ditch would be filled in.

And so all was well, but on Sunday morning the village streets were adorned with large printed posters:

> *"Comrades! Alleging as a pretext of offense the initiation of work of public utility, the reactionaries have staged an unseemly agitation that has offended our democratic instincts. On Sunday our borough is to receive a visit from the representative of a foreign power, the same in fact who has been indirectly the cause of the aforementioned agitation. Bearing in mind your just resentment and indignation, we are anxious to avoid, on Sunday, any demonstration which might complicate our relations with strangers. We therefore categorically exhort you to keep your reception of this representative of a foreign power within the limits of a dignified indifference.*
>
> *"Hurrah for the Democratic Republic! Hurrah for the Proletariat! Hurrah for Russia!"*

The streets were further enlivened by a throng of Party members who, it was easy to understand, had been specially mobilized with orders to parade the streets with *"dignified indifference,"* wearing red handkerchiefs or red ties.

Don Camillo, very pale around the gills, went into the church for a moment and was about to hurry away when he heard Christ calling him. "Don Camillo, why are you in such a hurry?"

"I have to go and receive the Bishop along the road," Don Camillo explained. "It is some distance, and then there are so many people about wearing red handkerchiefs that if the Bishop does not see me immediately he will think that he has come to Stalingrad."

"And are these wearers of red handkerchiefs foreigners or of another religion?"

"No, they are the usual rascals that You see before You from time to time, here in the church."

"Then if that is the case, Don Camillo, it would be better for you to take off that contraption that you have strapped on under your cassock and to put it back in the closet." Don Camillo removed the Tommy gun and went to put it away in the sacristy.

"You can leave it there until I tell you to take it out again," commanded Christ, and Don Camillo shrugged his shoulders.

"If I have to wait until You tell me to use a Tommy gun, we'll really be in the soup!" he exclaimed. "You aren't likely ever to give the word, and I must confess that in many cases the Old Testament . . ."

"Reactionary!" smiled Christ. "And while you are wasting time chattering, your poor old defenseless Bishop is the prey of savage Russian reds!"

This was a fact: the poor old defenseless Bishop was indeed in the hands of the agitators. From early morning, the faithful had flocked to both sides of the main road, forming two long and impressive walls of enthusiasm, but a few minutes before the Bishop's car was sighted, Peppone, warned by a rocket fired by his outpost to signal the approach of the enemy, gave the order to advance and by a lightning maneuver the red forces rushed forward half a mile, so that upon his arrival the Bishop found the entire road a mass of men wearing red handkerchiefs. People wandered to and fro and clustered into gossiping groups, displaying a "dignified indifference" toward the difficulties of the Bishop's driver who had to go at a snail's pace, clearing a passage by continuous use of his horn.

The Bishop, a bent and white-haired man whose voice when he spoke seemed to come not from his lips but from another century, immediately understood the *"dignified indifference"* and, telling his driver to stop the car, made an abortive movement to open the door. It appeared that he lacked the necessary strength. Brusco, who was standing near by, fell into the trap, and when he realized his mistake because of the kick Peppone had landed on his shin, it was too late and he had already opened the door.

"Thank you, my son," said the Bishop. "I think it would be better if I walked to the village."

"But it is some distance," muttered Smilzo, also receiving a kick on the shin.

"Never mind," replied the Bishop, laughing, "I wouldn't want to disturb your political meeting."

"It is not a political meeting," explained Peppone gloomily. "These are only workers quietly discussing their own affairs. You'd better stay in your car."

But by now the Bishop was standing in the road, and Brusco had earned another kick because, realizing that he was unsteady on his feet, he had offered the support of his arm.

"Thank you, thank you so much, my son," said the Bishop, and he set out, having made a sign to his secretary not to accompany him, as he wished to go alone.

And thus it was at the head of the entire red horde that he reached the zone occupied by Don Camillo's forces. And at the Bishop's side were Peppone, his headquarters staff, and all his most devoted henchmen because, as Peppone pointed out, the slightest gesture of discourtesy shown by any hot-headed fool to the representative of a foreign power would give the reactionaries the opportunities of their lives.

"The order remains and will remain unchanged," stated Peppone. *"Dignified indifference."*

The instant Don Camillo sighted the Bishop, he rushed toward him. "Excellency," he exclaimed, with great agitation. "Forgive me, but it was not my fault! I was awaiting you with all the faithful, but at the last moment . . ."

"Don't worry," smiled the Bishop. "The fault has been entirely my own. I took it into my head to leave the car and take a walk. All bishops as they get old become a little crazy!"

The faithful applauded, the bands struck up and the Bishop looked about him with obvious enjoyment. "What a lovely village!" he said as he walked on. "Really lovely, and so beautifully neat and clean. You must have an excellent local administration."

"We do what we can for the good of the people," replied Brusco, receiving his third kick from Peppone.

The Bishop, on reaching the square, noticed the large new edifice and was interested. "And what is that handsome building?"

"The People's Palace," replied Peppone proudly.

"But it is really magnificent!" exclaimed the Bishop.

"Would you care to go through it?" said Peppone while a terrific kick on the shins made him wince. That particular kick had come from Don Camillo.

The Bishop's secretary, a lean young man with spectacles perched upon a big nose, had caught up with the procession and now hurried forward to warn him that this was an unsuitable departure from routine, but the Bishop had already entered the building. And they showed him everything: the gymnasium, the reading-room, the writing-room, and when they reached the library he went up to the book shelves and studied the titles of the books. Before the bookcase labeled "Political," which was filled with propagandist books and pamphlets, he said nothing but only sighed, and Peppone, who was close to him, noticed that sigh.

"Nobody ever reads them," whispered Peppone.

He spared his visitor the inspection of the offices, but could not resist the temptation to show off the tea-room that was the object of his special pride, and thus the Bishop, on his way out, was confronted by the enormous portrait of the man with the big mustache and the small eyes.

"You know how it is in politics," said Peppone in a confidential voice. "And then, believe me, he isn't really such a bad egg."

"May God in His Mercy shed light upon his mind also," replied the Bishop quietly.

Throughout all this, Don Camillo's position was precarious. While he was indignant at the presumption upon the Bishop's kindness that inflicted on him an inspection of the People's Palace, which was a structure that surely cried to God for vengeance, on the other hand he was proud that the Bishop should know how progressive and up-to-date the village was. Moreover, he was not displeased that the Bishop should realize the strength of the local leftist organization, since it could only enhance the merits of his own Recreation Center in the Bishop's eyes.

When the inspection was at an end, Don Camillo approached the Bishop. "It seems a pity, Excellency," he said, so loudly that Peppone could not fail to hear him; "it seems a pity that our Mayor has not shown you the arsenal. It is believed to be the most fully supplied of the entire province."

Peppone was about to retort, but the Bishop forestalled him. "Surely not as well supplied as your own," he replied, laughing.

"That's no lie!" exclaimed Smilzo.

"He even has an S.S. mortar buried somewhere," added Brusco.

The Bishop turned toward Peppone's staff. "You wanted him back," he said, "and now you can keep him. I warned you that he was dangerous."

"He doesn't scare us," said Peppone with a grin.

"Keep an eye on him all the same," the Bishop advised him.

Don Camillo shook his head. "You will always have your joke, Excellency," he exclaimed. "But you have no idea what these people are like!"

On his way out of the People's Palace, the Bishop passed the bulletin-board, saw the poster and paused to read it.

"Ah," he remarked, "you are expecting a visit from the representative of a foreign power! And who may that be, Don Camillo?"

"I know very little about politics," replied Don Camillo. "We must ask the gentleman who is responsible for the poster. Mr. Mayor, His Excellency wishes to know who is the representative of a foreign power who is mentioned in your manifesto?"

"Oh," said Peppone, after a moment's hesitation. "The usual American."

"I understand," replied the Bishop. "One of those Americans who are looking for oil in these parts. Am I right?"

"Yes," said Peppone. "It's a downright scandal—any oil there may be belongs to the people."

"I quite agree," said the Bishop with the utmost gravity. "But I think you were wise to tell your men to limit their reactions to a *'dignified indifference.'* We would be foolish to quarrel with America, don't you agree?"

Peppone shrugged. "Excellency," he said, "you know how it is: one puts up with as much as one can and then comes the last straw!"

When the Bishop arrived in front of the church, he found all the local children from Don Camillo's Recreation Center in a neat formation, singing a song of welcome. Then an immense bouquet of flowers was presented to the Bishop by a small child with such beautiful curls and clothes that all the women nearly went out of their minds. There was complete silence while the infant, without pause and in a voice as clear and pure as a little spring of water, recited a poem in the Bishop's honor. After which everyone applauded the child, exclaiming that he was adorable.

Peppone went up to Don Camillo. "Dastard!" he hissed in his ear. "You take advantage of a child's innocence to make me ridiculous before everybody! I'll break every bone in your body. And as for that brat, I'll show him where he gets off. I'll chuck him in the river!"

"Good hunting!" replied Don Camillo. "Since he's your own son you can do what you want with him."

And it really was shocking, because Peppone carried the poor child off to the river like a bundle, and made him recite the poem in honor of the Bishop three times in a row.

THE BELL

Don Camillo, after a week during which he attacked Bigio at least three times daily wherever he met him, and shouted that he and all house-painters were robbers and lived only by extortion, had at last succeeded in agreeing with him on a price for whitewashing the outside walls of the rectory. And now, from time to time, he went to sit for a while on the bench in the church square to enjoy the spectacle of those gleaming white walls with the newly painted shutters and the climbing jasmine over the doorway.

But after each gratifying contemplation, Don Camillo turned to look at the church tower and sighed heavily, thinking of Gertrude.

Gertrude had been carried off by the Germans, and Don Camillo had fretted about her for nearly three years. Gertrude was the largest of the church bells, and only God could provide the necessary cash for the purchase of another bell of her majestic proportions.

"Stop brooding, Don Camillo," Christ said one day. "A parish can get along very nicely even if the churchtower lacks one of its bells. Noise is not everything. God has very sharp ears and can hear perfectly well even if He is called by a bell the size of a hazelnut."

"Of course He can," replied Don Camillo with a sigh. "But men are hard of hearing and it is to call them that bells are needed: the masses listen to those who make the loudest noise."

"Well, Don Camillo, peg away at it and you'll succeed."

"But, Lord, I have tried everything. Those who would like to give haven't the money, and the rich won't shell out even if you put a knife to their throats. I've been very near success with Sweepstakes tickets . . . A pity! If only someone had given me the shadow of a tip, just one break and I could have bought a dozen bells . . ."

Christ smiled. "You must forgive My carelessness, Don Camillo. You want Me in the coming year to keep My mind on the race? Are you also interested in the numbers game?"

Don Camillo blushed. "You misunderstood me," he protested. "When I said 'someone' I wasn't referring to You! I was speaking in a general way."

"I am glad of that, Don Camillo," said Christ with grave approval. "It is very wise, when discussing such matters, always to speak in a general way."

A few days later, Don Camillo received a summons to the villa of the Signora Carolina, and when he came home he was fairly bursting with joy.

"Lord!" he exclaimed, breathless before the altar. "Tomorrow You will see before You a lighted candle of twenty pounds' weight. I am going to the city to buy it and if they haven't got one, I'll have it specially made."

"But, Don Camillo, where will you get the money?"

"Don't You worry, Lord; You'll have Your candle if I have to sell the mattress off my bed to pay for it! Look what You have done for me!"

Then Don Camillo calmed down a little. "The Signora Carolina is going to give all the money needed for casting a new Gertrude!"

"And how did she come to think of it?"

"She said she had made a vow," explained Don Camillo, "to the effect that if the Lord helped her to bring off a certain business deal, she would give a bell to the church. Thanks to You, the deal was successful and within a month's time Gertrude will once more lift up her voice to Heaven! I am going now to order the candle!"

Christ checked Don Camillo just as he was taking off under full steam. "No candle, Don Camillo," Christ said severely. "No candle."

"But why?"

"Because I do not deserve it," replied Christ. "I have given the Signora Carolina no help of any kind in her affairs. If I were to intervene in such matters, the winner would bless Me while the loser would justifiably curse Me. If you happen to find a purse of money, I have not made you find it, because I did not cause your neighbor to lose it. You had better light your candle in front of the middleman who helped the Signora Carolina make a profit of nine million. I am no middleman."

The voice was unusually severe, and Don Camillo was filled with shame.

"Forgive me," he stammered. "I am a poor, dull, ignorant country priest and my brain is filled with fog and foolishness."

Christ smiled. "Don't be unjust to Don Camillo," He exclaimed. "Don Camillo always understands Me, and that is clear proof that his brain is not filled with fog. Very often it is precisely the intellect that fogs the brain. It is not you who have sinned; indeed your gratitude touches Me. But the Signora Carolina is neither simple nor honest, when she sets out to make money by enlisting God's help in her shady financial deals."

Don Camillo listened silently with his head bowed. Then he looked up. "I thank You, Lord. And now I shall go and tell that usurer that she can keep her money! My bells must be honest bells. Otherwise, it would be better to die without ever again hearing Gertrude's voice!"

He wheeled around, proud and determined, and Christ smiled as He watched him walk away. But as Don Camillo reached the door, Christ called him back.

"Don Camillo," said the Lord, "I know what Gertrude means to you, because I can always read your mind, and your renunciation is so fine and noble that it would purify the bronze of a statue of the Antichrist. Get out of here quickly or you will have Me granting not only your bell, but who knows what other devilment."

Don Camillo stood quite still. "Does that mean I can have it?"

"It does. You have earned it."

In such contingencies, Don Camillo invariably lost his head. As he was standing before the altar he bowed, spun on his heel, set off at a run, pulled himself up halfway down the nave and finally skidded as far as the church door. Christ looked on with satisfaction because even such antics can at certain times be a way of praising God.

And then, a few days later, there occurred an unpleasant incident. Don Camillo surprised an urchin busily working on the newly whitened walls of the rectory with a piece of charcoal. Don Camillo saw red. The urchin made off like a lizard, but Don Camillo was beside himself and gave chase.

"I'll collar you if I burst my lungs!" he yelled.

He started hot on the trail across the fields and at every step his ire increased. Then suddenly the boy, finding his escape blocked by a thick hedge, stopped, threw up his arms to shield his head and stood still, too breathless to utter a word. Don Camillo bore down on him like a tank and grasping the child's arm with his left hand, raised the other, intending dire punishment. But his fingers closed on a wrist so small and emaciated that he let go.

Then he looked more attentively at the boy and found himself confronted by the white face and terrified eyes of Straziami's son. Straziami was the most unfortunate of all Peppone's satellites, not because he was an idler—he was in fact always in search of a job, but because, once he found one, he would work quietly for one day and on the second he would have a fight with his employer, so that he seldom worked more than five days a month.

"Don Camillo," the child implored him, "I'll never do it again!"

"Get along with you," said Don Camillo abruptly.

Then he sent for Straziami, and Straziami strode defiantly into the rectory with his hands in his pockets and his hat on the back of his head.

"And what does the people's priest want with me?" he demanded arrogantly.

"First of all that you take off your hat or I'll knock it off for you, and secondly that you stop needling because I won't put up with it."

Straziami himself was as thin and as colorless as his son, and a blow from Don Camillo would have felled him to the ground. He threw his hat onto a chair.

"I suppose you want to tell me that my son has been defacing the Archbishop's Palace? I know it already, someone else told me. Your gray Eminence need not worry: this evening the boy will get a whipping."

"If you dare lay a finger on him, I'll break every bone in your body," shouted Don Camillo. "Suppose you give him something to eat! That wretched child is nothing but a skeleton."

"We aren't all the pets of the Eternal Father," began Straziami sarcastically. But Don Camillo interrupted him.

"When you do get a job, try to keep it instead of getting thrown out on the second day for spouting revolution!"

"You look after your own bloody business!" retorted Straziami furiously. He turned on his heel to go, and Don Camillo caught him by the arm. But that arm, as his fingers grasped it, was as thin as the boy's, so Don Camillo let go of it.

Then he went off to the altar. "Lord," he exclaimed, "must I always find myself taking hold of a bag of bones?"

"All things are possible in a country ravaged by so many wars and so much hatred," Christ replied with a heavy sigh. "Suppose you tried keeping your hands to yourself?"

Don Camillo went next to Peppone's workshop. "As Mayor it is your duty to do something for that unhappy child of Straziami," said Don Camillo.

"With the funds available, I might possibly be able to fan him with the calendar on that wall," replied Peppone.

"Then do something as chief of your beastly Party. If I am not mistaken, Straziami is one of your star scoundrels."

"I can fan him with the blotter from my desk."

"Heavens above! And what about all the money they send you from Russia?"

Peppone worked away with his file. "Stalin's mail has been delayed," he remarked. "Why can't you lend me some of the cash you get from America?"

Don Camillo shrugged his shoulders. "If you can't see the point as Mayor or as Party leader, I thought as the father of a son (whoever may be his mother!), you'd understand the need for helping that miserable child who comes and scribbles on my wall. And by the way, you can tell Bigio to clean my wall free of charge."

Peppone carried on with his filing for a bit, then he said, "Straziami's boy isn't the only child in the village who needs to go to the sea or the mountains. If I could have found the money, I would have set up a camp long ago."

"Then go and look for it!" exclaimed Don Camillo. "So long as you stay in this workshop and file bolts, Mayor or no Mayor, you won't get hold of money. The farmers are lousy with it."

"And they won't part with a cent, reverendo. They'd shell out fast enough if we suggested founding a camp to fatten their calves! Why don't you go to the Pope or to Truman?"

They quarreled for two hours and very nearly came to blows at least thirty times. Don Camillo was very late in returning.

"What happened?" Christ asked. "You seem upset."

"Naturally," replied Don Camillo, "when an unhappy priest has had to argue for two hours with a Communist Mayor in order to make him understand the necessity for founding a seaside camp and for another two hours with a miserly woman capitalist to get her to fork out the money for that same camp, he's entitled to feel a bit gloomy."

"I understand."

Don Camillo hesitated. "Lord," he said at last, "You must forgive me if I even dragged You into this business of the money."

"Me?"

"Yes, Lord. In order to compel that usurer to part with her cash, I had to tell her that I saw You in a dream last night and that You told me that You would rather her money went for a work of charity than for the buying of the new bell."

"Don Camillo! And after that you have the courage to look Me in the eye?"

"Yes," replied Don Camillo calmly. "The end justifies the means."

"Machiavelli doesn't strike me as sacred Scripture," Christ exclaimed.

"Lord," replied Don Camillo, "it may be blasphemy to say so, but even he can sometimes have his uses."

"And that is true enough," agreed Christ.

Ten days later when a procession of singing children passed by the church on their way to camp, Don Camillo hurried out to say good-by and to give out stacks of holy pictures. And when he came to Straziami's boy at the end of the procession, he frowned at him fiercely.

"Wait until you are fat and strong and then we shall have our reckoning!" he threatened.

Then, seeing Straziami, who was following the children at a little distance, he made a gesture of disgust. "Family of scoundrels," he muttered as he turned his back and went into the church.

That night he dreamed that the Lord appeared to him and said that He would sooner the Signora Carolina's money were used for charity than for the purchase of a bell.

"It is already done," murmured Don Camillo in his sleep.

FEAR

Peppone finished reading the newspaper and then spoke to Smilzo, who was perched on a high stool in a corner of the workshop awaiting orders.

"Go and get the truck and bring it here with the squadron in an hour's time."

"Anything serious?"

"Hurry up!" shouted Peppone.

Smilzo started up the truck and within three quarters of an hour he was back again with the twenty-five men of the squadron. Peppone climbed in, and they were very soon at the People's Palace.

"You stay here and guard the car," Peppone ordered Smilzo, "and if you see anything queer, shout."

When they reached the Assembly Room, Peppone made his report. "Look here," he said, thumping with his big fist upon the newspaper which bore enormous headlines, "matters have reached a climax: we are going to get it in the neck. The reactionaries have broken loose, our comrades are being shot at and bombs are being thrown against all the Party headquarters." He read aloud a few passages from the paper.

"And note that we are told these things not by one of our Party papers! This is an independent newspaper and it is telling the truth, because you can read it all clearly printed under the headlines!"

Lungo said that they ought to make the first move before the others got going—they knew every single reactionary in the district. "We ought to go to their houses one by one and pull them out and beat them up, and we ought to do it right now."

"No," Brusco objected, "that would put us in the wrong from the start. Even this paper says that we should reply to provocation but not invite it. Because if we strike, we give them the right to retaliate."

Peppone agreed. "If we beat up anybody, we ought to do it with justice and democratically."

They went on talking more quietly for another hour and were suddenly shaken by an explosion that rattled the windows. They all rushed out of the building and found Smilzo lying full length behind the truck, as though dead, with his face covered with blood. They handed the unconscious man to his family and leaped into the truck.

"Forward!" shouted Peppone, as Lungo bent to the wheel. The truck went off at full speed, and it was not until they had covered a couple of miles that Lungo turned to Peppone.

"Where are we going?"

"That's a good question," muttered Peppone. "Where *are* we going?"

They stopped the car and collected themselves. Then they turned around and went back to the village and drew up in front of the Demo-Christian headquarters. There they found a table, two chairs and a picture of the Pope, so they threw them out of the window. Then they climbed into the truck again and set out firmly for Ortaglia.

"Nobody but that skunk Pizzi would have thrown the bomb that killed Smilzo," said Pellerossa. "He swore he'd get even with us that time we had the fight during the strike."

When they reached the house, which was isolated, they surrounded it and Peppone went in. Pizzi was in the kitchen stirring the polenta. His wife was setting the table, and his little boy was putting wood on the fire.

Pizzi looked up, saw Peppone and immediately realized that something was wrong. He looked at the child who was now playing on the floor at his feet. Then he looked up again.

"What do you want?" he asked.

"They have thrown a bomb in front of our headquarters and killed Smilzo!" shouted Peppone.

"Nothing to do with me," replied Pizzi. The woman caught hold of the child and drew back.

"You said you'd get even. You reactionary swine!" Peppone moved toward him menacingly, but Pizzi stepped back and grabbing a revolver from the mantelpiece he pointed it at Peppone.

"Hands up, Peppone, or I shoot you!"

At that moment someone who was hiding outside the house threw open the window, fired a shot and Pizzi fell to the floor. As he fell his revolver went off, and the bullet buried itself among the ashes on the hearth. The woman looked down at her husband's body and put her hand in front of her mouth. The child flung himself on his father and began screaming.

Peppone and his men climbed hastily into the truck and went off in silence. Before reaching the village they stopped, got out and proceeded separately on foot.

There was a crowd in front of the People's Palace, and Peppone met Don Camillo coming out of it. "Is Smilzo dead?" Peppone asked.

"It would take a lot more than that to kill him," replied Don Camillo, chuckling. "Nice fool you've made of yourself throwing that table out of the window at the Demo-Christian headquarters. People are really laughing at that one."

Peppone looked at him gloomily. "There isn't much to laugh at, when people begin throwing bombs."

Don Camillo looked at him with interest. "Peppone," he said, "one of two things: you are either a crook or a fool."

Actually Peppone was neither. He just did not know that the

explosion had been caused by one of the retreaded tires of the truck, and a piece of rubber had struck the unfortunate Smilzo in the face. He went to look underneath the truck and saw the disemboweled tire, and then thought of Pizzi lying stretched out on the kitchen floor, of the woman who had put her hand to her mouth to stifle her screams and of the screaming child.

And meanwhile people were laughing. But within an hour the laughter died down, because a rumor spread through the village that Pizzi had been wounded.

He died next morning, and when the police went to question his wife the woman stared at them with eyes that were blank with terror.

"Didn't you see anyone?"

"I was in the other room; I heard a shot and ran in and found my husband lying on the ground. I saw nothing else."

"Where was the boy?"

"He was already in bed."

"And where is he now?"

"I've sent him to his grandmother."

Nothing more could be learned. Pizzi's revolver was found to have one empty chamber, the bullet that had killed him was identical with those remaining in the gun. The authorities promptly decided that it was a case of suicide.

Don Camillo read the report and the statements made by various persons that Pizzi had been worried for some time by the failure of an important deal in seeds, and had been heard to say that he would like to end it all. Then Don Camillo went to discuss the matter.

"Lord," he said unhappily, "this is the first time in my parish that someone has died to whom I cannot give Christian burial. And that is right enough, I know, because he who kills himself kills one of God's children and loses his soul and, if we are to be severe, should not even lie in consecrated ground."

"That is so, Don Camillo."

"And if we decide to allow him a place in the cemetery, then he must go there alone, like a dog, because he who renounces his humanity lowers himself to the rank of a beast."

"Very sad, Don Camillo, but so it is."

The following morning (it happened to be a Sunday), Don Camillo in the course of his Mass preached a terrible sermon on suicide. It was pitiless, frightening, and implacable.

"I would not approach the body of a suicide," he said in his peroration, "not even if I knew that my doing so would restore him to life!"

Pizzi's funeral took place that same afternoon. The coffin was followed by the dead man's wife and child and his two brothers in a couple of two-wheeled carts. When the family entered the village, people closed their shutters and peeped through the cracks.

Then suddenly something happened that struck everybody speechless. Don Camillo, with two acolytes and the cross, took his place in front of the hearse and preceded it on foot, intoning the customary psalms. On reaching the church square, Don Camillo beckoned to Pizzi's two brothers and they lifted the coffin from the hearse and carried it into the church, and there Don Camillo said the Office for the Dead and blessed the body. Then he returned to his position in front of the hearse and went through the village, singing. Not a soul was to be seen.

At the cemetery, as soon as the coffin had been lowered into the grave, Don Camillo drew a deep breath and said in a powerful voice: "May God reward the soul of his faithful servant, Antonio Pizzi."

Then he threw a handful of earth into the grave, blessed it and left the cemetery, walking slowly through the village, depopulated by fear.

"Lord," said Don Camillo when he reached the church, "have You any fault to find with me?"

"Yes, Don Camillo, I have. When one goes to accompany a poor dead man to the cemetery, one should not carry a pistol in one's pocket."

"I understand, Lord," replied Don Camillo. "You mean that I should have kept it in my sleeve so as to be handier."

"No, Don Camillo, such things should be left at home, even if one is escorting the body of a . . . suicide."

"Lord," said Don Camillo after a long pause, "I'll bet You that a commission composed of my most assiduous bigots will write an indignant letter to the Bishop, to the effect that I have committed a sacrilege in accompanying the body of a suicide to the cemetery."

"No," replied Christ, "I won't bet you, because they are already writing it."

"So now everyone in the village hates me—those who killed Pizzi, those who, while they knew like everybody else that Pizzi had been murdered, found it inconvenient that doubts should be raised regarding his suicide. Even Pizzi's own relations wanted it believed that he had killed himself. One of his brothers asked me: 'But isn't it forbidden to bring a suicide into the church?' Even Pizzi's own wife must hate me because she is afraid, not for herself but for her son, and is lying in order to defend his life."

The little side door of the church creaked, and Don Camillo looked round as Pizzi's small son entered. The boy came forward and stopped in front of Don Camillo.

"I thank you on behalf of my father," he said in the grave, hard voice of an adult. Then he went away as silently as a shadow.

"There," Christ said, "goes someone who doesn't hate you, Don Camillo."

"But his heart is filled with hatred of those who killed his father, and that is another link in an accursed chain that no one, not even You who allowed Yourself to be crucified, can break."

"The world has not come to an end yet," replied Christ serenely. "It has just begun and up There time is measured in millions of centuries. Don't lose your faith, Don Camillo. There is still plenty of time."

THE FEAR SPREADS

After the first issue of his parish magazine came out, Don Camillo found himself quite alone.

"I feel as though I were in the middle of a desert," he confided to Christ. "Even when there are a hundred people around me, there seems to be a thick wall that divides us. I hear their voices, but as though they came from another world."

"It is fear," replied Christ. "They are afraid of you."

"Of me!"

"Of you, Don Camillo. And they hate you. They were living warmly and comfortably in their cocoon of cowardice. They knew the truth, but nobody could compel them to recognize it, because nobody had proclaimed it publicly. You have forced them to face it, and because of that they hate and fear you. And if they were able, they would kill you. Does all this surprise you?"

Don Camillo shrugged. "No," he said. "But it would surprise me if I didn't know that You were crucified for telling people the truth. As it is it merely distresses me."

Presently a messenger from the Bishop came. "Don Camillo," he explained, "His Excellency has read your magazine and is aware of the reactions it has aroused in the parish. The first number has pleased him, but he doesn't want the second number to contain your obituary. You must see to it."

"That doesn't depend on the will of the publisher," replied Don Camillo, "and therefore any request of the kind should be addressed not to me but to God."

"That is exactly what the Bishop is doing," explained the messenger, "and he wished you to know it."

The police sergeant was a man of the world: he met Don Camillo by chance in the street. "I have read your magazine and the point you make about the tire tracks in the Pizzis' yard is very interesting."

"Did you make a note of this in your report?"

"No," replied the sergeant. "I didn't because as soon as I saw them I had casts taken. When I compared the casts with the various local cars, I discovered that those tracks had been made by the Mayor's truck. Moreover, I observed that Pizzi had shot himself in the left temple although he was holding the gun in his right hand, an awkward position at best. And when I searched in the fireplace, I found the bullet that was discharged from his revolver when he fell after being shot through the window."

Don Camillo looked at him sternly. "And why have you not reported all this?"

"I have reported it. And I was told that if the Mayor was arrested, the matter would immediately acquire a political significance. When such things get mixed up with politics there are complications. Therefore, I had to wait for an opportunity and you have supplied it. I was not evading my responsibility. I just didn't want this business to get bogged down because some people want to turn it into a political issue."

Don Camillo replied that the sergeant had acted very intelligently.

"But I can't detail two men to guard your back, Don Camillo."

"It isn't necessary, Sergeant. Almighty God will protect me."

"Let's hope He'll be more careful than He was of Pizzi," the sergeant retorted.

The following day, the inquiries were resumed and a number of landowners and leaseholders were rigorously questioned. Verola was among those called up for questioning and when he protested indignantly, the sergeant replied very calmly.

"My good sir: given the fact that Pizzi held no political views and belonged to no party, and that he was not robbed, and given also the fact that certain new evidence tends to suggest a murder rather than a suicide, we must exclude the supposition that we are dealing with either a political crime or a robbery. We must therefore direct our inquiries toward those who had business or personal relations with Pizzi and who may have borne him a grudge."

The matter proceeded in this way for several days and everyone questioned was furious.

Brusco was infuriated, too, but he held his tongue.

"Peppone," he said at last, "that devil is playing with us as though we were kids. You'll see—when he has questioned everybody he can think of, including the village midwife, he'll be coming to you with a smile to ask whether you have any objection to his questioning our men. And you won't be able to refuse, and he will begin his questioning and out will come the whole business."

"Don't be ridiculous," shouted Peppone. "Not even if they tore out my nails."

"It won't be you that they'll question, or me, or the others we are thinking of. They'll tackle the man who fired the shot."

Peppone jeered. "Don't talk rubbish! How can they when we don't even know who did it?"

And that was a good question because nobody had seen which of the twenty-five men of the squadron had fired the shot. When Pizzi fell they had all climbed into the truck and later on separated without exchanging a word. Since then no one had even mentioned the matter.

Peppone looked Brusco straight in the eyes. "Who was it?" he asked.

"Who knows? It could have been you."

"Me!" cried Peppone. "And how could I do it when I wasn't even armed?"

"You went into Pizzi's house alone and we couldn't see what you did there."

"But the shot was fired from outside, through the window. Someone must know who was stationed at that window."

"At night all cats are gray. Even if someone did see, by now he has seen nothing at all. But one person did see the face of the man who fired, and that was the boy. Otherwise his mother wouldn't have said that he was in bed. And if the boy knows then Don Camillo knows. If he didn't know he wouldn't have said or done what he has."

"May those who sent him here roast in hell!" bawled Peppone.

Meanwhile, the net was being drawn tighter, and every evening the sergeant came to inform the Mayor of the progress of the inquiries.

"I can't tell you more at the moment, Mr. Mayor," he said one evening, "but we know where we stand at last; it seems that there was a woman in the case."

Peppone merely replied: "Indeed!" But he would gladly have throttled him.

It was already late in the evening, and Don Camillo was thinking up jobs to detain him in the empty church. He set up a ladder on the top step of the altar. He had discovered a crack in the grain of the wood of the crucifix and after filling it, he was now applying some brown paint to cover up the repairs.

He sighed once and Christ spoke to him in an undertone. "Don Camillo, what is the matter? You haven't been yourself for several days. Aren't you feeling well? A touch of flu perhaps?"

"No, Lord," Don Camillo confessed without raising his head. "It's fear."

"You are afraid? But of what, in Heaven's name?"

"I don't know. If I knew what I was afraid of I wouldn't be frightened. There is something wrong, something in the air, something against which I can't defend myself. If twenty men came at me with guns I wouldn't be afraid. I'd only be angry because they were twenty and I was alone and without a gun. If I found myself in the sea and didn't know how to swim I'd think, 'There now, in a few minutes I'll drown like a kitten!' and that would bother me very much but I would not be afraid. When one understands a danger one isn't frightened. But fear comes with dangers that are felt but not understood. It is like walking with one's eyes bandaged on an unknown road. And it's a bad feeling."

"Have you lost faith in your God, Don Camillo?"

"No, Lord, the soul belongs to God, but the body is of the earth. Faith is a great thing but my fear is physical. I may have faith, but if I go for ten days without drinking I'll be thirsty. Faith consists in enduring that thirst as a trial sent by God. Lord, I am willing to suffer a thousand fears like this one for love of You. But still I am afraid."

Christ smiled.

"Do You despise me, Lord?"

"No, Don Camillo; if you were not afraid, what value would there be in your courage?"

Don Camillo continued to apply his paint brush carefully to the wood of the crucifix and his eyes were fixed upon the Lord's hand. Suddenly this hand seemed to come to life, and at that moment a shot resounded through the church.

Someone had fired through the window of the little side chapel.

A dog barked, and another answered; from far away came the staccato burst of a machine gun. Then there was silence once more. Don Camillo gazed with scared eyes into Christ's face.

"Lord," he said, "I felt Your hand upon my forehead."

"You're dreaming, Don Camillo." Don Camillo lowered his eyes and fixed them upon the hand. Then he gasped.

The bullet had passed through the wrist.

"Lord," he said breathlessly, "You pushed back my head and Your arm got the bullet that was meant for me!"

"Don Camillo!"

"The bullet is not in the wood of the crucifix!" cried Don Camillo. "Look where it went!"

High up on the right hung a small frame containing a silver heart. The bullet had broken the glass and had lodged itself exactly in the center of the heart.

"My head was just there," said Don Camillo, "and Your arm was struck because You pushed my head backwards!"

"Don Camillo, keep calm!"

But Don Camillo was beyond recovering his composure and if he hadn't promptly developed a high temperature, the Lord only knew what he might have done. And the Lord obviously did know, because He sent him to bed for two days with a fever that laid him as low and weak as a half-drowned kitten.

The window through which the shot had been fired looked out onto the little enclosed plot of land that belonged to the church. The police sergeant and Don Camillo stood there examining the church wall.

"Here is the proof," said the sergeant, pointing to four holes in the cement, just below the window sill. He took a knife from his pocket, dug into one of the holes and presently pulled out some object.

"In my opinion the whole business is quite simple," he explained. "The man was standing at some distance away and fired a round with his Tommy gun at the lighted window. Four bullets struck the wall and the fifth hit the window glass and went through it."

Don Camillo shook his head. "I told you it was a pistol shot and fired at close range. I am not yet so senile as to be unable to distinguish a pistol shot from a round of machine-gun fire! The pistol shot came first and was fired from where we are standing. Then came the burst from the Tommy gun from further away."

"Then we ought to find the empty cartridge near by!" retorted the sergeant. "And it isn't here."

Don Camillo shrugged. "You would need a music critic from La Scala to tell by the sound whether a shot comes from an automatic pistol or from a revolver! And if the fellow fired from a pistol he took the cartridge case with him."

The sergeant began to nose around and finally he found what he was looking for on the trunk of one of the cherry trees that stood in a row some five or six feet from the church.

"One of the bullets has cut the bark," he said and scratched his head thoughtfully. "Well," he said, "we might as well play detective!"

He got a pole and stuck it into the ground close to the church wall, in front of one of the bullet holes. Then he began to walk with his eyes fixed on the damaged cherry tree, moving to right or left until the tree was in a direct line with the pole by the wall. He found himself standing in front of a hedge. Beyond the hedge were a ditch and a lane.

Don Camillo joined him and they carefully examined the ground on either side of the hedge. They went on searching for a while and after about five minutes Don Camillo said: "Here it is," and held up a Tommy gun cartridge. Then they found the other three.

"That proves I was right," exclaimed the sergeant. "The fellow fired from here through the window."

Don Camillo shook his head. "I don't know much about machine guns," he said, "but I do know that bullets from other types of guns never describe a curve. See for yourself."

Just then a policeman came up to inform the sergeant that everyone in the village was quite calm.

"Isn't that nice!" remarked Don Camillo. "Nobody fires at them! It was me that got shot at!"

The sergeant borrowed the policeman's rifle and, lying flat on the ground, aimed in the direction of the upper pane of the chapel window where he thought the bullet had struck it.

"If you fired now, where would the bullet go?" asked Don Camillo.

"Unless it was a trained bullet, it couldn't have gone past the altar, not if it split itself in two!" said the sergeant. "Which only goes to show that anything you get mixed up in is always enough to make one tear one's hair! You couldn't be satisfied with one assailant! No, sir: you had to have two. One that fires from behind the window and another that fires from behind a hedge a hundred and fifty feet away."

"Oh well, that's the way I am," replied Don Camillo. "I never spare expense!"

That same evening Peppone summoned his staff and all the local Party officials to headquarters.

Peppone was gloomy. "Comrades," he said, "a new event has occurred to complicate the present situation. Last night some unknown person shot at the so-called parish priest, and the reactionaries are taking advantage of this to throw mud at the Party. The reaction, cowardly as always, has not the courage to speak out openly but is whispering in corners and trying to saddle us with the responsibility for this attack."

Lungo held up his hand and Peppone signed to him to speak.

"First of all," said Lungo, "we might tell the reactionaries that they had better offer proof that there really has been an attempt on the priest's life. Since there seem to have been no witnesses, the reverend gentleman himself might have fired off a revolver so he could attack us in his filthy periodical! Let us first of all get proof!"

"Right!" exclaimed his audience. "Lungo is perfectly right!"

Peppone intervened. "One moment! Lungo may be right, but we all know Don Camillo and we know that he doesn't use underhanded methods . . ."

Peppone was interrupted by Spocchia, the leader of the cell at Molinetto. "Comrade Peppone: do not forget that once a priest always a priest! You are letting yourself be carried away by sentimentality. Had you listened to me his filthy magazine would never have been printed and today the Party would not have had to put up with all the odious insinuations about Pizzi's suicide! There should be no mercy for the enemies of the people! Anyone who has mercy on the people's enemies betrays the people!"

Peppone crashed his fist down on the table. "I don't need any preaching from you!" he yelled.

Spocchia seemed unimpressed. "And moreover, if instead of opposing us you had let us act while there was still time," he shouted, "we shouldn't now be held up by a crowd of filthy reactionaries! I . . ."

Spocchia was a thin young man of twenty-five and sported an immense head of hair. He wore it brushed back, waved on top of his head and smooth at the sides, forming a kind of crest. He had small eyes and thin lips.

Peppone went up to him. "You are a half-wit!" he said, glaring. Spocchia paled but said nothing.

Returning to the table, Peppone went on speaking. "Taking advantage of the statement of a priest," he said, "the reaction is putting forward fresh speculations to the discredit of the people. The comrades need to be more than ever determined . . ."

Quite suddenly something happened to Peppone that had never happened before; he began listening to himself. It seemed to him as if he were in the audience hearing:

> *". . . and their bodies sold, the reaction paid by the enemies of the proletariat, the laborers starved . . . the lying clergy . . . the black government . . . America . . . plutocracy . . ."*

And as he listened he was thinking, "What does plutocracy mean? Why is that guy spouting about it when he doesn't even know what it means?" He looked around him and saw faces that he barely recognized. Shifty eyes, and the most treacherous of all were those of young Spocchia. He thought of the faithful Brusco and looked for him, but Brusco stood at the far end of the room, with folded arms and lowered head.

"But let our enemies learn that in us the Resistance has not weakened. . . . The weapons that we took up for the defense of our liberty . . ." And now Peppone heard himself yelling like a lunatic, and then the applause brought him back.

"Good work!" whispered Spocchia in his ear as they went downstairs. "You know, Peppone, just give the word and we could be ready in an hour."

"Swell!" replied Peppone, slapping him on the shoulder. But he felt like knocking him down, although he didn't know why.

He remained alone with Brusco and at first they were silent.

"Well!" exclaimed Peppone at last. "Have you lost your tongue? You haven't even mentioned my speech!"

"You spoke fine," replied Brusco. "Swell. Better than ever before." Then the silence fell between them.

Peppone was writing in a ledger. Suddenly he picked up a glass paperweight and threw it violently on the floor, bellowing a long, intricate and infuriated blasphemy. Brusco stared at him.

"I made a blot," explained Peppone, closing the ledger.

"Another of that old thief Barchini's pens," remarked Brusco, careful not to point out to Peppone that, as he was writing in pencil, the explanation of the blot did not hold up very well.

When they left the building and went out into the night they walked together as far as the crossroads and there Peppone stopped as though he had something that he wanted to tell Brusco. But he merely said: "Well, see you tomorrow."

"Tomorrow then, chief. Good night."

"Good night, Brusco."

TO MEN OF GOOD WILL

Christmas was approaching and it was high time to get the figures of the crèche out of their drawer so that they might be cleaned, touched up here and there and any stains carefully removed. It was late at night but Don Camillo was still at work in the rectory. He heard a knock on the window and, seeing that it was Peppone, went to open the door.

Peppone sat down while Don Camillo resumed his work, and neither of them spoke for quite a long time.

"Hell and damnation!" exclaimed Peppone suddenly and furiously.

"Couldn't you find a better place to blaspheme than in my house?" inquired Don Camillo quietly. "How about your own headquarters?"

"You can't even swear there any more," muttered Peppone. "Because if you do, someone asks for an explanation."

Don Camillo put a little white paint on Saint Joseph's beard.

"No decent man can live in this filthy world!" exclaimed Peppone after a pause.

"How does that concern you?" Don Camillo asked. "Have you by any chance become a decent man?"

"I've never been anything else."

"There now! And I never would have thought it." Don Camillo continued his retouching of Saint Joseph's beard. Then he began to tidy up the saint's clothing.

"How long will you be over that job?" asked Peppone angrily.

"If you'd give me a hand it would go quicker."

Peppone was a mechanic and he had hands as big as shovels and enormous fingers that gave an impression of clumsiness. But when anybody wanted a watch repaired they took it to Peppone. He could streamline the body of a car or the spokes of a wheel like a master painter.

"Are you crazy! Can you see me touching up saints?" he muttered. "You haven't by any chance mistaken me for your bellringer?"

Don Camillo fished in the bottom of the open drawer and brought out a pink and white object about the size of a sparrow: it was the Holy Infant.

Peppone never could remember how he came to find it in his hands, but he took up a little brush and began working carefully. He and Don Camillo sat on either side of the table, unable to see each other's faces because of the lamp between them.

"It's a rotten world," said Peppone. "If you have something to say, you don't dare trust anyone. I don't even trust myself."

Don Camillo seemed to be absorbed in his task: the Madonna's whole face required repainting.

"Do you trust me?" he asked casually.

"I don't know," said Peppone.

"Try telling me something and then you'll know."

Peppone completed the repainting of the Baby's eyes, which were the most difficult part. Then he touched up the red of the tiny lips. "I'd like to give it all up," said Peppone, "but it can't be done."

"What stops you?"

"Stops me? With an iron bar in my hand I could stand up to a regiment!"

"Are you afraid?"

"I've never been afraid in my life!"

"I have, Peppone. Sometimes I am frightened."

Peppone dipped his brush in the paint. "Well; so am I, sometimes," he said, and his voice was almost inaudible.

Don Camillo sighed. "A bullet was within four inches of my head. If I hadn't drawn my head back at that exact moment, I would have been done for. It was a miracle."

Peppone had completed the Baby's face and was now working with pink paint on His body.

"I'm sorry I missed," he mumbled, "but I was too far off and the cherry trees were in the way." Don Camillo's brush ceased to move.

"Brusco had been keeping watch for three nights around the Pizzi house to protect the boy—he must have seen who it was that fired at his father through the window, and whoever did it knows it. Meanwhile, I was watching your house because I was certain the murderer knew that you also knew who killed Pizzi."

"Who is he?"

"I don't know," replied Peppone, "I saw him from a distance creeping up to the chapel window. But I wasn't in time to fire before he did. As soon as he fired, I shot at him and I missed."

"Thank God," said Don Camillo. "I know how you shoot and we can say that there were two miracles."

"Who can it be? Only you and the boy can tell."

Don Camillo spoke slowly. "Yes, Peppone, I do know; but I cannot break the secrecy of the confessional."

Peppone sighed and continued his painting.

"There is something wrong," he said suddenly. "They all look at me with different eyes, now. All of them, even Brusco."

"And Brusco is thinking the same thing as you are, and so are the rest of them," replied Don Camillo. "Each is afraid of the others, and every time anyone speaks he feels as if he must defend himself."

"But why?"

"Shall we leave politics out of it, Peppone?"

Peppone sighed again. "I feel as if I were in jail," he said gloomily.

"There is a way out of every jail in this world," replied Don Camillo. "Jails can only confine the body and the body matters so little."

The Baby was now finished, and His bright coloring shone in Peppone's huge dark hands. Peppone looked at Him and he seemed to feel in his palms the living warmth of that little body. He forgot all about being in jail.

He gently laid the Baby on the table and Don Camillo placed the Madonna near Him.

"My son is learning a poem for Christmas," Peppone announced proudly. "Every evening I hear his mother teaching it to him before he goes to sleep. He's terrific!"

"I know," agreed Don Camillo. "Remember how beautifully he recited the poem for the Bishop!"

Peppone stiffened. "That was one of the most rascally things you ever did!" he exclaimed. "I'll get even with you yet."

"There is plenty of time for getting even, or for dying," Don Camillo replied.

Then he took the figure of the ass and set it down close to the Madonna as she bent over Her Child. "That is Peppone's son, and that is Peppone's wife, and this one is Peppone," said Don Camillo, laying his finger on the figure of the ass.

"And this one is Don Camillo!" exclaimed Peppone, seizing the figure of the ox and adding it to the group.

"Oh well! Animals always understand each other," said Don Camillo.

But Peppone said nothing, and for a time the two men sat in the dim light looking at the little group of figures on the table and listening to the silence that had settled over the Little World of Don Camillo and which no longer seemed ominous but instead full of peace.